The Bride Blog:
news of all things bridal.

Wedding-dress designer Chloe's shocking video confession: she never really believed in love.

After three failed engagements, did wedding-dress designer Chloe Allen put a secret curse on all her gowns, so that no one else would get a happily-ever-after, either?

The question on the minds of brides-to-be everywhere: How could anyone marry in a Chloe gown and ever think their love will last?

Word is that brides are storming Chloe's showroom in Brooklyn, demanding to return their dresses and to get their money back, much like the old-fashioned run on a failing bank.

How long can the House of Chloe hold out? Time will tell, dear brides. Time will tell.

Dear Reader,

Some time ago, I became obsessed over the sheer number of wedding dresses for sale on Craigslist. (I'm a writer. We do odd things like that.) Were people just not staying married anymore? And dumping their poor dresses, too? Or were they never making it down the aisle? Had they maybe found other dresses they liked better, after already buying one?

Were they young married couples, broke and really needing money? Was there no sentiment left about the wedding dress?

And then I started to think...what if you were the designer of those dresses, and suddenly, all of these women started returning your beautiful gowns? It might look like the problem wasn't the women, but the wedding dresses....

Which is when I discovered Chloe, a wedding-dress designer who fears she's cursed in love. Which is a real problem, because nobody wants to buy a wedding dress from a designer who's cursed in love.

Teresa Hill

HIS BRIDE
BY DESIGN

TERESA HILL

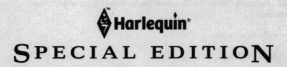

Harlequin®

SPECIAL EDITION

If you purchased this book without a cover you should be aware that this book is stolen property. It was reported as "unsold and destroyed" to the publisher, and neither the author nor the publisher has received any payment for this "stripped book."

PLEASE RECYCLE • THIS PRODUCT IS RECYCLABLE

Recycling programs
for this product may
not exist in your area.

ISBN-13: 978-0-373-65624-0

HIS BRIDE BY DESIGN

Copyright © 2011 by Teresa Hill

All rights reserved. Except for use in any review, the reproduction or utilization of this work in whole or in part in any form by any electronic, mechanical or other means, now known or hereafter invented, including xerography, photocopying and recording, or in any information storage or retrieval system, is forbidden without the written permission of the publisher, Harlequin Enterprises Limited, 225 Duncan Mill Road, Don Mills, Ontario M3B 3K9, Canada.

This is a work of fiction. Names, characters, places and incidents are either the product of the author's imagination or are used fictitiously, and any resemblance to actual persons, living or dead, business establishments, events or locales is entirely coincidental.

This edition published by arrangement with Harlequin Books S.A.

For questions and comments about the quality of this book please contact us at Customer_eCare@Harlequin.ca.

® and TM are trademarks of Harlequin Books S.A., used under license. Trademarks indicated with ® are registered in the United States Patent and Trademark Office, the Canadian Trade Marks Office and in other countries.

www.Harlequin.com

Printed in U.S.A.

TERESA HILL

tells people if they want to be writers, to find a spouse who's patient, understanding and interested in being a patron of the arts. Lucky for her, she found a man just like that, who's been with her through all the ups and downs of being a writer. Along with their son and daughter, they live in Travelers Rest, South Carolina, in the foothills of the beautiful Blue Ridge Mountains, with two beautiful, spoiled dogs and two gigantic, lazy cats.

If I had to list all the poor people who had to listen to me
whine over the writing of this book—
while also moving from a house we'd lived in for
eighteen years and sending our baby girl off to college—
the list would probably be longer than the book.

But you all know who you are, and I thank you sincerely
and say once again, I'm sorry, truly sorry.
Couldn't have done it without you all.

Chapter One

Dreams did come true.

People had always told Chloe Allen that, but she hadn't quite believed it until the lights in the tent went down, the music rose and she had the world of New York fashion at her feet. If they loved her designs, Chloe would get absolutely everything she ever wanted.

"I think I'm going to throw up," she whispered to her cousin and first assistant, Robbie, who'd been hovering by her side the whole morning. Her business manager and accountant, Addie, who she claimed as a sister, was in the back somewhere, as was Robbie's twin, Connie, her second assistant. This was truly a family business.

"You can throw up later," Robbie said. "Right now, you have to do one last check of the models and start the show, before something happens."

"What do you mean, something happens? Something bad?"

Because Chloe felt it. Even standing in the dark, surrounded by the models in all her beautiful dresses ready
to walk that runway, she felt like something bad was coming.

Robbie gave her a little shove to the spot by the entrance
to the runway, thrusting her into the spotlight, and from
there it was all a blur until it was time to send the last dress
down the runway. Eloise, the snottiest model of all, stood
before Chloe, pouting that usual model pout, except it always seemed extra-pouty when aimed at Chloe. She took
off, doing that odd, abrupt model strut, the dress in ecru-
colored silk charmeuse swishing and swaying beautifully
as she walked down the runway.

The crowd was on its feet, cheering madly.

Chloe started to cry, couldn't help it.

She'd done it!

The models lined up and took one more turn around
the runway, all together. Chloe fell into step behind Eloise
and her pretend groom, who as Chloe understood it was
actually Eloise's boyfriend of the moment.

They got to the spot where Chloe's fiancé, Bryce, a
fashion photographer, stood covering the show, and their
friends in the audience started calling for Bryce to join
Chloe on the runway. He jumped up there, lean and fashionable in black jeans and a plain black T-shirt, smiling
that dazzling Bryce smile, giving Chloe a kiss on the
cheek. They stood at the end of the runway with Eloise
and her model groom/boyfriend, cameras flashing from
all directions.

Chloe finally started to breathe, to let it all sink in. The
show had gone off without a hitch, the audience applaud-
ing wildly!

Then she felt Eloise fidgeting, heard a quiet hiss of sharp
words. Chloe shot her a glance that said, *Surely this can*

wait until we're off the runway! Eloise's boyfriend whispered back furiously, Bryce, too. People started to notice, falling silent and then whispering themselves.

Not now. Not now. Not now! Chloe chanted to herself.

"You bastard!" Eloise screamed, but not at her boyfriend. At Bryce? "You just couldn't keep your hands to yourself, could you?"

Chloe whimpered, all the breath going out of her in a rush.

Her fiancé was involved with her top model?

It was such a cliché, especially finding out while standing here at the end of the runway, like making it all the way down the aisle of a church to the altar only to find disaster. This was supposed to be Chloe's day. Didn't they understand? She was the real bride here!

Eloise shook a long, pointy finger in Bryce's face. "I told you to stay away. I told you I wouldn't stand for this anymore."

Bryce looked pale and defeated. Chloe's mind had gone foggy and sluggish. Eloise was telling Bryce to stay away? So, Bryce was like...annoying Eloise? Stalking her?

Laughter trickled in, getting louder and louder, and then the camera flashes became positively blinding. Chloe stood frozen in the midst of it.

Then she realized that Eloise didn't seem to be trying to keep Bryce away from her. She'd planted herself between Bryce and her model boyfriend/groom, shrieking, "He's mine!"

That couldn't be right.

Bryce was sexy as could be, and somehow he'd become Chloe's. He wanted her, despite spending his days photographing some of the most beautiful women in the world, unreal and yet gorgeous in that odd, perfect way of theirs.

Chloe caught a look passing not between Bryce and

Eloise, but Bryce and the male model. The ridiculously toned, tanned, good-looking male model.

An intimate, knowing, regretful look.

Which meant…

"Oh, no," Chloe whispered, fighting with all she had in her not to cry. Not here. Not now.

Chloe, wannabe wedding dress designer extraordinaire, part of the big machine that made little girls' wedding dreams come true, had a fiancé who was sleeping with another man!

James Elliott IV did not in any way keep up with fashion news.

His idea of fashion was—when he was feeling really daring—to forego his traditional white dress shirt in favor of one in pale yellow or perhaps blue.

But one fine September morning, as he walked from his apartment in Tribeca to his office in the financial district and stopped to buy his *Wall Street Journal* at his favorite newsstand, it was impossible to miss the fashion news. It was plastered across the front pages of the tabloids for all to see.

Some crazy model in a huge, billowing wedding dress jumping a guy on a runway, looking like she was about to claw his eyes out in the next instant.

Waiting for his turn to pay, James decided the model did indeed look crazy, but then most of them were, he suspected. Starvation made women mean and at least a little bit crazy. The photo showed that she had literally jumped on the guy, had her legs wrapped around his waist and her fingernails poised and ready to strike, the guy twisting to get out of the way.

In the background was a model in a tux, looking like he

wanted to jump in, but didn't have the balls to do it. And down at the bottom, in the foreground…it looked like…

"Chloe?"

She was his ex.

The ex, if he let himself admit it. The one who'd really gotten to him, endearing herself to him like no one else, infuriating him, baffling him, hurting him, until they'd finally gone their separate ways.

What the hell had happened to Chloe?

The headline on the tabloid read Taking Bridezilla to a Whole New Level: Bloodshed at Fashion Week as Eloise Goes on a Rampage!

Bridezilla?

And who was Eloise?

The next tabloid blared Wedding Dress Designer Chloe and Model Eloise's Man-on-Man Nightmare! Their Men Cheating… With Each Other!

James grimaced on Chloe's behalf.

And the third said Designer Chloe's Fashion Week Debut Every Woman's Wedding Nightmare: The Groom-to-Be Prefers Men!

Now James felt really bad.

There'd been a time right after their breakup when he'd been mad enough to want Chloe's heart broken, but this seemed unreasonably harsh. If it was even true. Most of the stuff in these rags wasn't, after all.

"Mr. Elliott?" The puzzled voice of the newspaper vendor, Vince, interrupted him. "You want one of those tabloids today?"

"What?" He looked at the man who'd been selling him financial news for years. Nothing but financial news. "Of course not. I was just…waiting to pay."

Vince shrugged like he didn't believe a word of it, then said, "Hot story this morning. We usually don't get anything good that normal people care about during Fashion Week. But a girl-on-girl brawl over two men…that's hot!"

"Chloe and that model got into it?"

"Who?"

"The wedding dress designer."

"Yeah." Vince nodded enthusiastically. "Right there on the runway, I heard. Hope somebody got video. I could get into that. You know that girl? Chloe?"

"Used to," he admitted. What the hell? It was Vince. They were morning newsstand buddies.

"She looks kind of mousy in most of the pictures," Vince said. "Like that Eloise chick could tear her apart if she wanted to."

James would never have said Chloe was mousy. She liked to pretend she was tough as nails and incredibly self-sufficient, especially when it came to her career. But when it came to her personal life, she could be sweet, gentle, vulnerable at times, fun, full of life, until she drove a man absolutely crazy. None of that equated to mousiness.

Although he had to admit, in the brawl photos, she looked tiny and sad standing there dejectedly on the sidelines. It looked like her show had been ruined, and she'd been working her whole life for a chance like that. She'd wanted it more than she'd wanted him, that was for sure. And it had just burned him up at the time.

"Sure you don't want one of those?" Vince asked, pointing at the tabloids. "They've got more pictures inside."

"No, thanks." No way he was going to buy that on the street. He'd swipe his assistant's copy.

Strolling into his office on the twenty-sixth floor, he greeted his secretary and his secretary's secretary and then asked Marcy, his assistant, to come into his office, a large, starkly bare room with a massive, gleaming wooden

desk, big, cushy leather chairs and an expansive view all
the way down to New York Harbor and Battery Park.

He believed in order, discipline, control, hard work and
the power of his own mind. People called him a financial
genius, and he just smiled and went on with his work.
While the current times were challenging, they certainly
hadn't caught him by surprise, and he was doing just fine
while others around him floundered. Never believe the
hype about anything—especially the economy—he always told people. The philosophy had served him well.

He wondered now if he'd hyped the whole idea of Chloe
in his mind to an impossible level. He couldn't have been
as happy with her as he remembered or as miserable without her, he told himself.

And he wasn't obsessing.

Just…curious.

"Mr. Elliott? Are you feeling all right?" Marcy asked.

"Of course," he claimed, then couldn't quite bring himself to ask for what he really wanted. He cleared his throat,
adjusted his tie, frowned. "I just…I need…I want to see
your copy of the *New York Mirror*."

Marcy sputtered. Her eyes got all big and round and
then her cheeks turned red. "But I don't—"

"Oh, yes, you do. I know you have that thing, and I want
it—"

"But why?"

"You know why. I'd bet a thousand dollars you know
exactly why."

She looked truly flustered then, but didn't deny either
having the damned thing or knowing why he wanted it.
She'd come to work for him in the immediate post-Chloe
era. He'd been in a truly ugly mood for weeks, and had
ended up springing for unscheduled bonuses to her and a

handful of other staff members forced to put up with him, as a way of saying he was sorry.

"Okay. I'll go get it," Marcy said, turning on her heel and heading out.

"And don't you dare tell anyone!" he yelled as she opened the door, his secretary and his secretary's secretary peering through, looking worried.

Great. Just great.

Marcy came back with the tabloid carefully rolled up tightly so no one could see what it was. At least she was embarrassed to have it. She scowled as she handed it to him, then reached over to type something into his computer.

"You'll want the tabloid for the photos, but the best written account is here." She pointed to a blog now up on his computer screen, then retreated from his office in an embarrassed huff.

James glanced through the tabloid photos, grimacing at what he saw, then turned to the blog.

The Bride Blog: News of all things bridal.

Bridal Brawl Breaks Out at NY Fashion Week!

Talk about a Bridal Nightmare!

Forget the bridesmaids! It's the other men modern-day brides have to worry about, as we saw in the amazing brawl that broke out at New York Fashion Week.

Wedding dress designer Chloe Allen, plucked from obscurity mere months ago when gorgeous pop star Jaden Lawrence got married in a Chloe gown, was having her first showing at Fashion Week when everything suddenly went horribly wrong.

It seems Chloe's fiancé, veteran fashion photographer Bryce Gorman, just couldn't keep his hands off the male model posing as the groom to model extraordinaire Eloise's bride at what was to be the climax of the show.

And what a climax it turned out to be!

One doesn't think of models like the beautiful Eloise as the kind to ever worry about losing a man to anyone, but lose him she did, and she clearly put the blame on Bryce Gorman.

Eloise jumped him—literally—designer wedding gown and all. She wrapped those incredibly long legs around his waist and held on tight, her long, pale pink fingernails clawing at his face, supposedly drawing blood.

Bryce swung around trying to dislodge her, as her long train and veil floated around them in an odd mélange of satin, lace and bridal horror that will not soon be forgotten.

So far the only video clips of the scene have been particularly unsatisfying. (A free bridal bouquet to the first person who sends a good video of the bridal brawl to this blog.)

Meanwhile, traumatized brides, especially the ones closest to their big day, have been writing to the Bride Blog like mad to say they're keeping a close eye on those groomsmen and any close friends of their grooms.

It seems that old nightmare of standing at the altar, surrounded by friends and family, and finding out at the last minute that the groom had a little fling with one of the bridesmaids has been replaced with the modern-day equivalent.

The groom doing another man!

* * *

Chloe woke from her post-apocalyptic haze the day after the show, praying it had all been a horrible nightmare and that she could do it all over again. Even for her—a woman who liked to think of herself as highly creative—the previous day had been outlandishly bad.

She looked up and there was Addie, whom Chloe claimed as a half sister, although no one had ever done the paternity tests to be sure. Chloe's father had slept with Addie's mother at about the right time, and that was enough for the two of them, who found each other much more reliable than their father.

"Tell me it didn't really happen," Chloe begged.

"Oh, honey. I wish I could." Addie sat down on the bed, her back against the headboard, offering Chloe a shoulder if she needed it.

Chloe leaned her head on Addie's shoulder and thought this had to be the absolute worst day of her life. Yesterday had been horrible, but her family had closed in around her, gotten her out of the tent and then poured drinks down her throat until everything became a blur.

Today, she didn't have the luxury of alcohol or denial. "I thought he was the one," she cried.

"I know, sweetie."

Addie, kindly, did not point out that Chloe always believed every new man in her life was *the one*. She wasn't stupid, just ever hopeful. At least that's what Chloe tried to tell herself. Although after being engaged three times and never making it to the altar, it was getting harder and harder to believe.

Her family loved weddings. They married over and over again. And the wedding was always the high point. All their relationships went downhill from there. Chloe thought she was breaking the pattern thus far by not marrying, but even that hadn't protected her from her own unique wedding curse.

There was Fiancé No. 1, her high school sweetheart. Chloe liked to think they'd merely been too young to know what they wanted, no giant failure there or any kind of sign.

Bryce, No. 3, was sexy, fun, confident and in the business, someone who understood exactly what it took to be a success. He had come along at the perfect time.

When Chloe was just getting over No. 2.

Addie said that timing was the only reason Chloe ever gave Bryce the time of day, but Chloe truly didn't think so. She wouldn't fall for one man to the point of becoming engaged to him—all just to get over another man, would she?

No. 2—although he would absolutely hate being thought of as second in anything—was James Elliott IV, one of the most eligible bachelors in New York, according to several magazine lists. Chloe didn't talk about No. 2.

"Wait a minute," Addie said, pouncing on her. "You're not even thinking about Bryce. You're thinking about… the other one!"

"Am not," Chloe claimed.

"You are so!"

"Well, now I am! Why did you have to say that?"

"Because you got that look. That look you only get when you're thinking about him! About—"

"Don't say it! Don't you dare say his name!"

"About good old No. 2," Addie said, looking quite smug about it.

"Haven't I been through enough humiliation already?" Chloe asked. "Without going into my long list of failures with men?"

"True," Addie agreed. "Sorry."

Chloe frowned. She hadn't even gotten out of bed yet, and already the day looked bleak. While her personal life might be truly disastrous, she'd always been so much better at managing her professional life. The fact that the two had now become entwined, her personal life mess spilling over into a huge career mess, was more than a little unsettling.

"Okay, how bad is it this morning?" Chloe asked. "Everyone saw…everything yesterday?"

"And got pictures, I'm afraid," Addie admitted.

Chloe groaned, seeing the explosion of camera flashes in her face once again.

"There are people who claim all publicity is good publicity," Addie tried.

"You've never been one of those people," Chloe reminded her.

"I could have been wrong about that all this time."

Not likely, but Chloe loved her for saying so.

"Okay, here it is." Addie spilled the ugly truth: "You're front-page news in all the tabloids today."

Chloe winced.

"A feat normally achieved only by celebrities and politicians in the midst of major sex scandals," she added.

"And here I never set that as one of my career goals."

"On the bright side, your name is out there once again."

"Except now I've designed a dress for a wedding nightmare—"

Addie looked horrified. "Don't say that! Don't you ever say that! Women get a little crazy about their weddings. A little…weird and controlling and fanatical and superstitious. You know that! They're all worried some disaster will strike."

"Exactly. And when they think of getting married in a Chloe original, they'll think disaster, guaranteed!"

"Chloe, I swear, never, ever say that again. Do you hear me? It's like tempting the Wedding Gremlins to attack."

"They already attacked! I mean, my fiancé was doing the groom. What else could possibly happen?"

"Oh, my God!" Addie crossed herself in horror. "Never, ever, ever, ever say that! The moment women start to believe your dresses are bad luck, you're dead as a wedding dress designer. We are happy people who sell wedding dreams. We believe in love, fairy tales, happily-ever-afters and all that crap."

"Okay!" Chloe said obediently. She could always count on Addie for a pep talk. "Sorry. I just had a bad moment, but I'm done now."

"Fine, but it can't go out of this room."

"Of course not," Chloe said, then had a flash of her sobbing, drinking and talking to someone. She had that same really icky feeling she'd had before the runway show, when she just knew something would go wrong.

Had she done something last night? Other than have a little too much to drink and cry a bit? She didn't think so, but she really couldn't remember.

Must have been a bad dream, she decided.

After all, her fiancé was sleeping with the groom.

What could possibly top that?

Addie left, and Chloe lay there in her bed a moment longer, working up the courage to face the day. Weariness weighed her down. She let her eyes drift shut and her mind float into that never-never land between real sleep and a groggy kind of wakefulness.

She was at the bar, last night but not really last night. She'd laughed, cried, gone over her entire, dreary history with men, and then, just when things seemed their bleakest, she'd looked to the end of the bar, and *he'd* been there.

Not Bryce.

James.

Chloe groaned, half in pain and half in longing, knowing she was crazy even for dreaming of him.

He looked so good. But then, James always had.

He could have been a model himself, although he hated to hear it. In fact, they'd met when Chloe had mistaken him for a model late for one of her shows. He had that rare quality of being an absolutely beautiful man, but still looking unmistakably masculine, as so few models did.

In the bar, he walked over to her, looking at her with the kind of understanding and concern that made her ache. Then he reached out with one of those perfect hands of his and wiped away her tears. And in the kindest move of all, put his beautiful body between her and the rest of the room, creating a tiny, safe space for her when she was so miserable she just wanted to curl up into a little ball and disappear.

He smelled so good, the way he always did. He'd admitted with a reluctance that bordered on pain that he still thought about her, that he missed her and that he just had to come see for himself that she was all right.

It was ridiculous.

Even in her dream, she realized that.

James Elliott was too proud, too stubborn and too independent to ever admit he missed anyone. But it was a lovely dream, bittersweet and achingly real.

Then she woke up once again, not twenty minutes later, in her bed, yet still very much inside her very own nightmare as fashion runway roadkill.

James fought the impulse all day, but nightfall found him standing on the corner across the street from the big, old Victorian near Prospect Park in Brooklyn that Chloe shared with her various relatives, who all worked for her in the first-floor showroom.

He stared up at the window of the small attic she'd turned into a tiny apartment for herself, where she had some measure of privacy. This after fighting with himself all day about coming anywhere near here.

It felt weirdly stalkerish to be there, just looking up at her window, and he was a man who did not stalk women. He just needed to know she was okay.

Which he couldn't tell from simply staring at her house.

Still, he felt a little better, just being this close to her.

He waited until the last light went out in her little attic, saw the slightest impression of her, he thought, ghostlike against the sheer curtains, as she walked across the room. He imagined her climbing into bed, her toes cold, letting her warm them on his, his hands hot against her cool, pale skin, tangling in her glorious hair.

So many nights they'd spent that way, together in that room.

He couldn't have her back, he told himself.

He'd made her crazy, and she'd done the same to him. He was as logical a man as there was on earth, and he knew without a doubt that no one needed to be hurt like that a second time.

So once the light was out, and he knew she was safe in her bed, at least for the night, he turned around and went home, swearing to himself that he wouldn't be back.

Chapter Two

The next morning, James faced the newsstand, hoping to see the usual mix of tabloid headlines screaming about drunken celebrities, corrupt politicians, alien sightings and baseball players on steroids.

No such luck.

That crazy model, Eloise, was back on the covers, in handcuffs, still wearing the wedding dress, her hair going every which way, mascara-streaked tears on her cheek, maybe a few drops of blood on the gown? The bridezilla label had been picked up by every tabloid he saw, now in this humongous font with letters the color of blood.

James winced as he stood there. *Bridezilla?* Had someone climbed a skyscraper in a bloody wedding gown and swatted at things? He didn't think so.

What about Chloe? He scanned the news. Supposedly in a fit of rage, she'd destroyed every gown in her showroom with a huge pair of scissors. No way James believed that.

She loved the clothes she made too much to ever destroy them, and Chloe didn't do *fits of rage.* She just didn't.

James got to the front of the line to hand over his money for his *Wall Street Journal,* and Vince said, "Your girl is back."

"Yeah, I see that."

"One of my customers just told me about this great video of the whole runway brawl," Vince confided. "YouTube, that thing the kids like on the computer? Type in 'Runway Brawl,' and it's supposed to come right up."

James nodded. He wouldn't be able to help himself. "I'll do that, Vince."

When he got to the office, he glared at Marcy, then gave a curt nod for her to follow him into his office. "People are online watching a video of the brawl at Chloe's show?"

"More than a hundred thousand people so far," Marcy said.

James grimaced. A hundred thousand? "Someone's keeping a count?"

"Of course. At the rate the video's being downloaded, it could go viral at any time."

Which would be bad for Chloe. "We need to stop that from happening."

"You can't stop it. It's already out there. It has a life of its own now."

"There has to be a way," he argued.

Marcy shrugged. "Maybe if Angelina Jolie actually left Brad Pitt or something equally earth-shattering."

James sighed. "I guess we can't make that happen."

"I can't. Unless you know how to find them, and you want to make a play for Angelina. I guess if you wanted me to do my best to seduce Brad…I mean, if you ordered me to, I'd have to do it for you."

James considered. "You're telling me you'd seduce Brad Pitt for me?"

"I'm a team player, sir," she claimed.

"Well, it's good to know you're willing, Marcy, if it ever comes to that."

"Yes, sir." Marcy made a face. "I'm afraid there's something else you need to know. Adam Landrey called. He said to tell you Chloe's company needs another infusion of cash."

James tried not to show anything in his face. "How much?"

"Six figures, at least." Marcy clearly disapproved. "You broke up with the woman, sold your interest to your friend, then guaranteed he wouldn't lose any money on the deal? You guaranteed his losses?"

"What if I did?" James argued.

"The two of you broke up!" Marcy repeated.

"I remember. Very well, thank you." He glared at her. "Your point?"

"Are you going to treat me this well if I leave you?" Marcy asked. "Because I've never had a guy be that nice to me after I left him."

"Leave me now, Marcy, or you might find out how badly I'll treat you."

She made a face, but left his office, closing the door behind her.

James went for the computer, found the video as easily as Vince said he would. It was like rubbernecking a particularly brutal car accident, except this accident involved someone he knew. Poor Chloe.

He picked up the phone to call Adam. When James and Chloe had broken up, she'd wanted him out, as an investor, immediately, and people weren't lining up to take a risk in the fashion industry. James felt bad about the way things ended between them. He felt guilty and couldn't bear to see her lose her design business, too. The only way he could get someone to take over his investment was to guarantee any losses the new investor might suffer.

Something Chloe would definitely not be happy about, even now, if she found out. It made James sound like some kind of controlling, overbearing, interfering man—all of which she'd accused him of being, when all he'd been trying to do was help. He was, after all, a brilliant business-man. What kind of a fiancé would he be if he didn't help her? Chloe was brilliant herself, but creatively, fashion-ably. She didn't have a businesslike bone in her body.

But all that was old news. Chloe should definitely be old news to him.

As long as nothing else really bad happened, she would be.

The Bride Blog: News of all things bridal.

Wedding Dress Designer Chloe's Shocking Video Confession: She Never Really Believed in Love.

After three failed engagements, did she put a secret curse on all her gowns? So that no one else gets a happily-ever-after, either?

The question on the minds of brides-to-be every-where: How could anyone marry in a Chloe gown and ever think their love will last?

Word is that brides are storming Chloe's show-room in Brooklyn, demanding to return their dresses and to get their money back, much like the old-fashioned run on a failing bank.

How long can the House of Chloe hold out?

Time will tell, dear brides.

Time will tell.

Addie was scared to go downstairs that morning. They hadn't actually had *hordes* of angry brides demanding refunds so far, but they'd had enough to scare Addie. What would they find today, after the latest Bride Blog piece, and a new video of Chloe, drunk in the bar the night of the bridal brawl, talking about her diastrous three engagements and claiming she never believed in love? Chloe even described herself as "cursed in love" in the new video. So Addie was scared to even look outside.

She crept into the showroom without turning on any of the lights and peeked out between the window blinds in the corner farthest from the door, and there stood…one, two, three hysterical-looking brides already, bridal garment bags in hand, no doubt the much-feared, supposedly cursed wedding dresses inside, ready to be returned.

"Oh, my God!" Addie cried, then crept away from the window, for fear that they would see her.

They weren't even supposed to open the store until noon. This was the day they stayed open until 8:00 p.m., for brides-to-be who worked all day, and it was barely 9:00 a.m. now. They were about to be overrun, all because of that stupid Bride Blog woman!

James wasn't surprised later that morning to see Adam looking a little uncomfortable across the breakfast table, saying he was sorry, but he just couldn't put any more money into Chloe's business right now. Another friend had already clued James in to the fact that Adam himself was not in the best financial shape at the moment. Hardly anyone was.

"I'll take care of it." James held out a checkbook for his personal account.

"If that's what you want." Adam looked like he was dying to ask what James was doing, bailing out a woman who'd dumped him a year and a half ago.

Fair question, and not one James cared to answer for anyone, not even to himself. He shrugged, tried to play it off and said, "She's great in bed."

Adam looked like he didn't believe that reason at all, but volunteered, "I wouldn't know about that."

"Good," James said, ridiculously happy to hear it.

"I mean, she's adorable, funny, seems very sweet, obviously unusually talented and driven when it comes to her work."

James nodded. She was. What could he say? He hated the idea of her being hurt, of her losing her business, losing her dream. Other than that…he just didn't know.

As James handed his check to Adam, Marcy burst in, looking absolutely petrified. "There's a riot at Chloe's!"

James gaped at her. "Riot!"

Marcy nodded frantically. "That Bridal Blog lady? She said there's a riot breaking out at Chloe's store right now. Disgruntled brides storming the place, wanting their money back for the cursed dresses. It's all over Twitter. I thought you'd want to know right away."

He did. He'd ordered Marcy to keep him updated on the Chloe situation. But now that he knew this, he should probably run in the opposite direction. His life had gotten weird from the moment she came back into it. Not that she was truly in his life again. It just felt like it. From the distance of cyberspace, his favorite corner newsstand and that one night on the street corner across from her house, she was having her strange effect.

And he was afraid he liked it. He'd liked it the first time.

Life had been interesting, surprising, even felt a little… fun. He could have that again. She was in trouble, and he was going to help her. Crazy as it was, it was what he'd wanted from the moment he'd looked up and seen her face on those stupid tabloid covers.

"I'm going over there," he said, feeling better than he had in ages.

Now that James had given in, he couldn't get to Chloe fast enough.

"She makes me a little crazy," he confessed to Adam, who'd gotten into the taxi with James, probably to see just how crazy James was. Over a woman.

"Chloe's a very interesting person," Adam said carefully.

"She is. I just need to make sure she's okay," James claimed, which was so obviously a lie. He was acting like a madman over her.

"Hey, I like Chloe. She's great," Adam began.

"You swear you never slept with her?" James just couldn't help but ask.

"I swear. My life is screwed up enough—"

He broke off as James scowled at him.

"I mean, complicated. My life is really complicated. The last thing I need is to get involved with any woman. Even one as interesting and cute as Chloe."

"Okay," James said, satisfied for the moment on that count.

After about twenty minutes, he looked out the car window, and there, a block away, was Chloe's shop, that huge, old Victorian where she lived with her two cousins and Addie. He saw some kind of commotion out front and two, no, three camera crews and some of those big, tall lights the TV people used when they filmed things.

James charged into the mass of crazy, garment-bag-wielding brides, just as one of them drew back to take a swing at Chloe, who looked like a waif in her pajama bottoms and one of those stretchy little spaghetti-strap tops she liked to sleep in.

He thought those were the sexiest things he'd ever seen.

Especially when she wore one of those tops and nothing else except a little scrap of lacy panties. Chloe at her softest, most inviting, rumpled best.

God, he'd missed her!

Just then, another bride took a swing at her with her garment bag. The blow sent her stumbling backward. James stepped in and caught her hard against him, feeling a huge surge of relief, just having his arms around her. She went limp like she suddenly didn't have any bones and looked absolutely stunned, either from the blow or seeing him, he couldn't be sure. He lifted her up into his arms, glaring at the garment-bag-slinging woman, daring her or anyone else to come close to Chloe now that he had her.

Chloe reached out a hand to ever so lightly touch the side of his face, like she needed to know he was real. "James?"

"It's okay," he said, tucking her face against his chest, trying to reassure himself that she was truly okay. "I've got you."

When he lifted his head, he realized the crowd had quieted, finally.

They were all staring at him and her, and he realized there were a few still photographers there and that they were clicking away at the scene.

He didn't care.

"What the hell is going on here?" he asked, spotting Chloe's half sister, who'd always been the sanest one of the family.

"They want their money back for their dresses," she said, glaring at him.

"Write them checks, if that's what it takes to get them to leave," he said.

"I'll take care of it," said Adam, who'd fought his way to James's side. Adam, who had a check James had just written in the car, a check with lots of zeroes on it. Let everyone think Adam was covering the new debts, too. James would find a way to explain exactly what was going on to Chloe later.

His first thought was to get her away from this crowd, inside, maybe even carry her upstairs to her cute, quirky attic apartment, where he'd bumped his head on the low, sloped ceilings more than once. To the big cream-colored iron bed he used to share with her.

He hesitated, wondering if he was making a mistake by not taking her to his apartment in the city. Here she could kick him out whenever she pleased. When she got her second wind, she'd start her whole I-don't-need-anyone routine. But he couldn't risk giving this mob a second chance at her. That settled it. He took her inside.

Reluctantly, he set Chloe on her feet just inside the doorway. She seemed so slight standing there in front of him, so sad and defeated. He put his hand to the side of her face, tilting it up toward the light.

"Is it just this?" he asked, finding a slight swelling at her cheekbone. "Or are you hurt anywhere else?"

"I'm fine," she insisted.

But her face was pale as could be, a few tiny, light brown freckles that he knew she hated spread across her nose and cheeks. He used to tease her that her freckles looked like fairy dust and kiss each one. God, he'd lost his head completely over this woman the first time and was clearly in danger of doing the same thing again.

He couldn't help it.

He leaned down, his face lingering against hers, the tip of his nose pressed against her skin, soaking in the sweet, wild essence of Chloe, drawing his other hand through her pretty blond hair. It was even longer than it used to be and hanging loose and messy, the way he remembered it from rare mornings when she'd arisen from her bed before he left.

She was not a morning person, had always said she did her best work late at night. He didn't mind. It was fine to get up and dressed and be able to stand there and stare at her in a rumpled bed, her hair all wild around her face, those little sprinkles of fairy dust on her bare cheeks.

How had he ever managed to drag himself away?

How would he do it again?

Was he not going to think of saving himself from her a second time? Self-preservation was usually one of his strong suits. But he just couldn't bring himself to care at the moment.

He picked her up once again and carried her upstairs.

Chloe was still thinking it all had to be a dream.

Monkeys escaped from zoos at times and attacked people. Bears walked out of the woods and into camping areas. Every now and then an elephant got loose from its ankle stakes.

But who got attacked by crazy, garment-bag-wielding brides?

Didn't happen.

She'd never heard of it happening, never read about it, never imagined it. What made it even more improbable was that James Elliott IV would show up, charge into the crowd and rescue her from them. Yet, in her muddled mind, that's what had happened.

He laid her gently on the unmade bed in her little attic apartment, then sat down by her side, looking concerned and strong and tall and absolutely gorgeous.

She whimpered and then said, "Pinch me."

He frowned, touched his hand to the side of her face, feeling the spot where she thought the shoes in one of the brides' garment bags had gotten her. "Do you need a doctor? I'll take you."

"No, I mean…I think I'm dreaming…" Then thought how that might sound to him.

I was dreaming you came charging to my rescue, after a year without a word from you….

No, not going there.

Not with James, especially if he really was here.

"I dreamed I was being attacked by brides with bouquets," she said.

Which had him looking even more concerned. "Flowers? Chloe, those were garment bags—"

"No, I know that! I'm just confused," she said. "Not in that concussion sort of way. In that this-is-really-weird kind of way. You know?"

"Yes," he agreed, still looking worried.

God, he smelled so good, so familiar.

Chloe winced.

Not now. Her life was falling apart already. She could not do this now with him. She looked at him warily.

Collapsing in his arms the minute she saw him again was not how she'd ever imagined any reunion they might have. She was supposed to look her best, maybe all done up for a show, and he was supposed to look bleak and sad and lonely without her. He was supposed to say he missed her terribly, that he had never stopped thinking about her.

That's how it was supposed to go.

"All of that really happened just now?" she asked him.

"Yeah, it did."

"Pinch me," she said. "I have to be sure."

James smiled for the first time since she'd seen him again, looking heartbreakingly sexy and so appealing she thought about dragging him down into the bed with her right that minute.

"I'm not going to pinch you," he whispered, ever so slowly lowering his head to hers.

Her whole body started trembling before he even touched her, and she could have stopped it. Truly, she had time. And some sense of self-preservation that was still alive inside of her.

After all, her most recent ex-fiancé had just been outed as a sometimes-gay man, having an affair with Chloe's model's boyfriend, outed on the runway at her Fashion Week show. Even Chloe, stupid as she could be about men, knew that the last thing she needed was for James Elliott to kiss her, even just once.

But he'd charged to her rescue like Prince Charming, saving her from hysterical, rioting brides, after all. She still wasn't convinced this was real. So she let him kiss her. It wasn't the stupidest thing she'd done lately, and it was one thing she actually wanted to happen.

He let his whole body sink into hers, those chiseled abs, the hard chest, wide shoulders. They sank into the feather mattress on her bed like they used to do. He'd loved this bed with her in it. She whimpered, a rush of hurt and longing washing over her, sending her arms around his shoulders and pulling him closer.

"Don't be scared," he said, tenderly, sweetly, his mouth merely a breath from hers.

And then he finally closed that last bit of distance between them, his lips soft and firm, heartbreakingly familiar, and yet as tentative as he'd ever been with her. As if he knew how much this meant to her, and he truly didn't want to hurt her. As if he knew what they were both risking, and yet just couldn't stop himself.

She let her eyes drift shut, drew in that wonderful man scent of his. Her hands came up to frame his face, to slide into his hair. He had beautiful, thick black hair. He took his time with the kiss, didn't attack with his mouth as so many men did. He coaxed. He soothed. He smiled against her mouth, teasing ever so softly with his tongue, while she wanted to open up and devour him whole.

He had to know that.

It had always been that way between them.

He took little nibbles of her, her mouth, her ear, her neck, back to her mouth, so carefully, so sweetly, with a kind of power and control that drove her crazy at the same time it left her in complete awe of him.

He could seem so cool, so reasonable, so strong. Was this some sort of game to him, a corporate takeover he'd planned out in minute detail and executed to perfection? But then she caught a glimpse of his face, his eyes, and she saw. He was burning up inside, as desperate for her as she was for him.

Was he still desperate for her? Had he missed her? Thought about her? Could he possibly want her back? At this, the worst moment in her life?

She lay there beneath him, in complete awe, her head still spinning, that perfect, hot, hard body of his pressing into hers, which was positively purring with pleasure.

He'd finally stopped teasing. Now he was kissing her for real, his body thrusting ever so slightly against hers in time with the thrust of his tongue in her mouth, everything about this, about him, as exciting as ever.

He could have her clothes off in seconds. She knew it. She could be naked beneath him, wrap her legs around him, open herself up to him in every way, and he could be inside of her, hers again, at least for a few moments. She wanted it, and so did he.

It would be so easy, and so good.

And then they'd be right back to where they'd started, everything that had gone wrong between them still there for them to deal with. She couldn't trust him. She knew it. She'd caught him with a model named Giselle, seen it with her own two eyes, and that had finally been the end of her and James.

Chloe drew in a big breath of him, of everything he was, everything she felt, everything she'd missed so much about him, and somehow found the strength to turn her head away, to break the kiss, kill the moment.

He went still on top of her, slowly raised his head and looked down at her, passion blazing from his dark, beautiful eyes, along with a million questions. And he had that dazed look that had her thinking he was as confused as she was.

Had this really happened? Were they sure it wasn't all a dream? A bizarre but very good one?

"You saved me from the brides?" she asked tentatively.

He cocked his head to the side, looking truly worried, then carefully, slowly, raised himself off her to sit by her side. His hand came to her face, tenderly working its way over her head, his eyes searching.

"Chloe, are you hurt?"

"No," she whispered. "Not really. I was dreaming about my show. Did you see the video? It's all over the internet. Everyone's watching."

"Yes, I saw it."

"The way Bryce kept turning in a circle to try to get away from Eloise's fingernails, and how her veil floated around them in circles, so you saw the whole thing through this gauzy haze, even the blood?"

"Yes."

"If they made horror movies for fashion designers and brides, that's what it would look like."

"Chloe, you're scaring me," he said.

"And that dress? I loved that dress. I loved it more than any other dress I've ever designed, because I looked great in that dress. That was going to be my wedding dress. Why did it have to be that dress Eloise was wearing when it happened?"

"I don't know, Chloe. I'm really sorry. About everything."

"All I have left is the sleeve. Bryce grabbed at Eloise to get her off of him, and all he got was the sleeve. He just ripped it off the dress. Robbie found it on the runway after everyone left and brought it back to me. It's all I have."

"You made it once. You can make it again," he tried.

"No. Not after what happened. It's cursed, too, like me."

"Chloe, you are not cursed," he insisted. "You know that."

"My poor dress. Do you think it ended up in jail with Eloise? Because I just hate thinking about that beautiful dress being dragged across that filthy floor at the jail. Do you think maybe you can bail a dress out of jail? And leave the person wearing it there?"

"Chloe?" He looked really scared then, like she was freaking him out. She tried to get up, but he wouldn't let her. "Not now, okay? The brides are still downstairs. We need to wait a while, until they leave."

"Okay. I don't want to see them again. They were mean brides."

"Chloe, did any of them hit you? Other than the one

who got you here?" He touched her poor cheek. "Did anyone hit your head?"

"I don't think so."

"Do you know where you are?"

"I think so." She was with him, in her bed, even though
that made no sense. "In my house. In my bed."

He smiled encouragingly. "Good. You scared me for a
minute."

So it had happened. It was real.

"I don't understand," she whispered.

Why was he here? Why did he care? Why was he being so nice to her? Why had he kissed her like that? She
thought he hated her, if he felt anything at all for her anymore. She'd hated him as best she could for as long as she
could, because that was the best way to get over him, to
try to forget him. Not that it had worked all that well.

"Chloe, have you been getting any sleep the last few
days?" he asked, looking like he wanted to haul her off to
the hospital and have her head examined, at the very least.

"Not much," she admitted. "I keep having nightmares.
Very strange nightmares."

"Okay, maybe you just really need to sleep," he said,
forcing a smile. "How about this? You stay here, close your
eyes, and I'll stay right here until you go to sleep."

He took a couple of pillows and piled them up against
the headboard, kicked off his shoes, pulled off his tie and
suit coat, then sat down on her bed, settling her against
his side, her head against his chest.

"I just…I don't understand," she said one more time.

"I know. Just go to sleep. I won't let anything bad happen to you."

It was the sweetest, most welcome thing he could have
offered her. Rest, peace, safety, with him right beside her,
watching out for her, just like in her dream.

* * *

He waited until she was asleep, and then waited a little bit longer, taking it all in. Being in her bed again, kissing her, holding her, wanting her so bad he ached with it. The smell of her, the joy, the absolute chaos, all still there, all just the same.

Except she was more vulnerable now than she'd ever been, and he'd come charging in like a man who had every right to be here and to protect her, sweeping her off her feet and fighting his way through a frenzied matrimonial mob to save her.

It was the charging-in thing, the every-right-to-be-there thing she'd most certainly object to, once she wasn't dazed and sleep-deprived and maybe concussed. He hadn't been able to find any evidence of a head injury, but she certainly seemed a little out of it, even for Chloe.

James was tempted to stay with her, but he had no idea what might still be happening with the riot downstairs. So, though it was the last thing he wanted to do, he disentangled himself as gently as he could, leaving her asleep, curled up against a pillow instead of him. He tucked covers around her like she was a child who needed to be protected from the cold, smoothed down her hair, kissed her forehead.

Then he dragged himself away.

Downstairs in the kitchen he found Addie and Chloe's twin cousins, Robbie and Connie. Adam was still there, too.

They all looked up as James entered, giving him the thorough once-over. Too late, he straightened his tie, smoothed down his jacket and then his hair, trying not to look like a man who'd just crawled out of bed. *Oh, well.*

"Is she all right?" Addie asked finally, clearly having a hard time believing what she was seeing.

James nodded. "She's asleep. Did she get hit on the head?"

They discussed it for a moment, then determined that no one had actually seen Chloe take such a blow.

"She was confused," James said.

"She might still think this whole morning was a nightmare," Robbie said, then looked at James, and mouthed, "I didn't mean seeing you, exactly, was a nightmare—"

"It's all right," James said.

Had she kissed him back only because she'd thought she was dreaming and been confused about who he was? James had no way of knowing, so he concentrated on the business at hand.

"You took care of that crazy mob?" he asked.

Addie nodded, looking from James to Adam and then back to James, like she knew they were both up to something. "We wrote a lot of checks."

"Okay," James said, as if that settled that. If there was going to be a fight about the money, it was between him and Chloe, no one else. "I think you should post a security guard outside for the next day or so. You don't know if you've reached the end of the crazy brides. We don't want anyone getting hurt."

He realized, too late once again, that it wasn't his decision to make, and looked at Adam to save him.

"I was thinking the same thing," Adam said. "I'll just have to find—"

"I know someone," James said, pulling out his phone. "Good guy."

"Good," Adam said. "Thank you."

Addie had obviously heard enough. She turned to James and asked, "What are you doing here?"

"I was…with Adam," James said. "We were having a business meeting nearby when we heard about the riot at

Chloe's. Adam was concerned, so he came over to make sure everyone was okay. And I came with him. That's all."

"That's all?" Addie laughed out loud. "What did you do to Chloe?"

"I just got her away from the mob out front and brought her upstairs to rest. Nothing more."

"And she just fell asleep?" Robbie was indignant now.

"I didn't hurt her," he claimed. "I wouldn't do that."

But he had.

They knew it. He knew it, too.

She hurt me, too, dammit.

He thought it, but didn't say it.

"She's perfectly fine," he insisted. "Just a little confused, and she said she hadn't been getting much sleep since the runway thing."

"You know about the runway thing?" Addie asked.

"Half the solar system knows about the runway thing," he said, which was true. He just wasn't normally in the half that followed tabloid news. But still… "Just let her rest. I'm going to call the security guy I know."

"I won't leave until a guard gets here," Adam offered.

James was so grateful for the out, he could have kissed Adam for offering, but then everyone might think that for some reason every man Chloe was involved with eventually turned to other men, and that was publicity she certainly didn't need. So James merely thanked Adam and left.

He'd lost his mind tonight.

That was the only explanation possible for all of this.

He went back to his office and forced himself to work until midnight, then went home and tossed and turned until he finally fell asleep.

Chapter Three

Chloe had no idea how long she slept, waking, if possible, even more disoriented than before. She'd barely turned over in her bed to squint at the clock, when her bedroom door opened slowly, quietly.

Addie and Robbie peeked in, whispering furiously to each other.

"I'm awake," she said.

They nearly tripped over each other getting inside, then just stared at her like she might have dropped in from a spaceship or something. She looked down at herself in the bed. She was in her favorite sleep attire, cotton spaghetti-strap camisole and pajama bottoms, nothing out of the ordinary about that.

"What?" she finally asked.

"She's dressed in her PJs," Robbie said. "He wouldn't... you know...and then dress her again afterward."

"Maybe he didn't take the time to undress her at all,"

Addie argued. "It's not like it's completely necessary. Maybe he's that kind of guy. You know. In. Out. Done. Over. Outta here."

"I bet he's better than that. You know. You can tell—"

"I can't tell. How do you tell just from looking that a guy will take the time to undress you completely first?"

And then it was all starting to come back to Chloe.

The crazy brides with the bouquets, but really with garment bags, probably with shoes in them, because they were heavy. Especially when people were swinging them at her. And then…then…

"Oh, my God! He was here?" she cried.

Addie and Robbie fell silent and solemn, just looking at her.

She started gasping for breath. "I think I might hyper-ventilate. He was really here?"

They nodded.

"He saved me from the rioting brides?"

"He did," Robbie confirmed. "It was like something out of *Gone with the Wind*. Rhett and Scarlett on the stairs and all."

"James Elliott was here, and he carried me up the stairs? To my room? This room?" She tried breathing faster and faster, conscious but in that fuzzy-headed way of one who's slept too long and can't really wake up.

"We followed as soon as we could," Robbie said.

James must have been here for a while. She vaguely remembered him touching her softly, sweetly, his body pressing hers down into the mattress, his mouth on hers, just as hot and sexy as ever.

Chloe lifted up the covers and peeked beneath them at herself. Yes, she was completely dressed, and he was definitely a man to completely undress a woman in those kinds of situations, though she wasn't confirming or denying any of that to Addie or Robbie.

So, he'd just kissed her? And held her? And then left?

"How long was he in my room with me?" she asked finally.

"Thirty-seven and a half minutes," Robbie said.

They'd timed the visit? Of course.

"We were thinking of breaking in—"

"Because we thought…I don't know, maybe you'd lost your mind or something, and we should try to save you from yourself," Addie finished. "Should we have been saving you from yourself?"

"Probably. Yes." Then she had a new, even more horrible thought. "He knew why those crazy brides were here?"

"Oh, yeah."

She looked up into their equally worried faces and felt anew the sinking feeling of complete humiliation. Not just the rest of the known world, but James, too, knew her ex No. 3 had a thing for men, and he'd been here to witness the aftermath of her latest disastrous relationship.

"What in the world was he doing here?" she asked finally.

"He said he was having a business meeting with Adam Landrey when they heard about the riot. Adam was here, too," Addie told her.

"I still can't believe it. It doesn't make any sense."

He was here? Yes, she could still smell him in her bed. That fresh, clean, citrusy smell of him. She thought she could feel his arms around her, her body snuggled up to his, could remember feeling safe and cherished and so turned on. Why would he charge in, rescue her from the crazy brides and then carry her up here and kiss her? Then leave without a word?

Addie frowned at her. "He thought you might have been

hit in the head, that you were a little out of it, a little confused."

Oh, perfect. At least she had an excuse for whatever she'd done.

"Do you need a doctor?" Robbie asked.

"A mental-health professional. We should probably keep one on call."

James was whistling as he approached the newsstand the next morning, then saw that Vince was waiting for him, tabloid in hand.

Uh-oh. Did they have photos of the mob scene from Chloe's?

But as he got closer, he saw that Vince was beaming at him. "Today, it's on the house! This and your *Wall Street Journal*."

This, it turned out, was a tabloid with a cover shot of him saving Chloe from the mob!

"You're the first one of my regulars to make the cover of a periodical I carry!" Vince said. "How 'bout that? I've been telling everybody this morning that I know you, that I see you here every day!"

James groaned and looked again. Could anyone—except maybe people who saw him every day—tell that was him? In the photo, his head was bent down toward Chloe's as he carried her through a sea of rioting brides. She looked like a waif, a beautiful, fragile, helpless waif. And he was mostly just a dark suit with dark hair, he thought.

"So, you and that designer get back together?" Vince asked.

"Not exactly."

"Hey, come 'ere." Vince motioned for James to lean

over the counter, closer to Vince, who'd pulled out his cell phone and held it out in front of them.

"No!" James pulled away as the flash went off. He could only hope he'd gotten out of the way in time. "No pictures. Not today."

Vince looked mightily disappointed. "I was gonna put it up on the newsstand. You know, to show people that I really know you."

"Yeah. I'm just not ready for that, Vince. And I really hate having my picture taken," he said.

"You date that crazy girl, you're gonna get your picture taken."

He hadn't thought of that when he'd charged to her rescue, but he couldn't really say he regretted it, either. Because he'd gotten to see her again, to hold her again, to kiss her. He'd gotten into her bed again. He grinned at that thought. Not in the way he'd really like to be back in her bed, but it was certainly better than not being anywhere near her bed.

"I gotta ask you," Vince said, grinning wickedly. "Once you carried her off like that, what did you do to her then?"

"Nothing," James claimed. "Absolutely nothing."

"Yeah, right," Vince said.

A gentleman didn't kiss and tell, after all, and he prided himself on being a gentleman.

He got to his office to see Marcy waiting for him, looking as freaked out as he'd ever seen her and carrying a rolled-up copy of a tabloid.

"Let me guess." James went into his office, Marcy following. "You've never worked with anyone who made the cover of a tabloid before?"

Her mouth fell open. "You've seen it?"

"If it's the one I'm thinking of, I have. Please tell me I didn't make the cover of more than one?"

"No, just the one." She laid it down in front of him on his desk. "We're probably going to start getting calls—"

"From the tabloids? They know who I am?"

"Suspect, at least. The Bride Blog piece yesterday did mention you by name in connection with Ms. Allen, and if we're going to get calls, I need to know what to say."

She waited, looking so eager and excited.

"You mean, you want me to tell you what happened yesterday?"

"Only so I can do my job," she claimed.

Yeah, right. She was practically salivating at the thought of getting the tabloid news before anyone else.

"There is something seriously wrong with you, Marcy," he said.

"I know. Believe me, I do. I'm so sorry. Everyone has a weakness, a dirty little secret, and this is mine."

And Chloe was his.

His weakness, but not his secret. Not anymore. He didn't think he'd left any room for doubt about how he felt about her.

"She was in trouble, and I helped her out. That's it. End of story. I'm not going to stand by and watch anyone I know get attacked." He made it sound perfectly reasonable, he thought, like he was some sort of freelance do-gooder.

Marcy didn't look like she was buying a word of it. She'd seen him charge out of the restaurant like a crazy man to get to Chloe yesterday, after all.

"So, that Bride Blog thing yesterday…I never actually saw it."

"You're not going to like it," Marcy warned, handing

him a printout with the pertinent parts highlighted in yellow.

He scanned the article. It referred to him as Fiancé No. 2 and mentioned that stupid eligible bachelor list he'd been on, then got to the she-just-wanted-him-for-his-money part.

Well, that hurt.

Still.

He'd hurled that particular accusation at her after they broke up. Sometimes he believed it, sometimes he didn't, but it still had the power to make him seriously annoyed.

"Well, I've never been happy being No. 2 in anything," he said, handing that piece of trash back to Marcy. "And please tell me they're wrong about that stupid bachelor list. I can't be on that thing again!"

Marcy looked a little nervous. "The Single Woman's Guide to Bachelor Hunting in New York? I called. I'm afraid you're going to be on it again."

James cringed. He'd made *New York Woman*'s annual bachelor list for the first time a few weeks before he and Chloe had gotten engaged. Truly rotten timing, because women could be so aggressive these days. They'd been all over him. It had been a constant annoyance and a major source of tension between him and Chloe. So once again, this was the worst possible timing.

"What do I have to do to get off that stupid list?" he asked.

"Lose all your money or get married," she said, demonstrating that logical Marcy was still in there somewhere. "Or I guess you could leave New York."

No good options there. "Maybe we could just buy the stupid magazine and do away with the list."

Marcy paused, pen and pad in hand, like she wasn't sure whether she should write that down or not.

"I'm not that desperate yet. Still, there has to be something we can do."

"Well, it seems obvious. You need a girlfriend," Marcy advised.

"No, I don't." He was still smarting from the last one. *Chloe.*

"A very public girlfriend," Marcy insisted. "Take her out, smile for the photographers, just as that stupid list comes out. That way, women will think you're taken and leave you alone."

No, they wouldn't. He was painfully aware of that. Of course, it might be even worse, even more women, more aggressive, if he appeared to be completely available.

"I guess that would be less of a hassle than buying the damned magazine. When does the issue come out?"

"Next week. You'll have to date fast."

A very public girlfriend?

One of those women who needed three hours to pull herself together to walk out the door, who wanted every moment of her life gossiped about, speculated about and, best of all, captured on film.

Which made him think about Chloe. Vince had said that morning, *Date her, you're going to get your picture taken.*

Chloe as his very public, fake girlfriend.

As if reading his mind, Marcy continued. "You've already got a good start on it. Your rescue of Ms. Allen was like something out of a fairy tale." She sighed heavily. "It played very well in the blogs today, the way you took her in your arms and fought to get her to safety. People already want to know about the two of you."

Marcy got a particularly dreamy look on her face. James didn't want to admit that Chloe's behavior might be attributable to a slight blow to the head that left her disoriented. It would ruin the whole fantasy—fairy tale element, and he'd seldom seen Marcy look so happy—and maybe a little goofy.

He feared he'd looked the same way when he'd finally seen Chloe the day before—just plain goofy-giddy-stupid with happiness. Hopefully Chloe was too confused to remember.

"Marcy, come back to me," he said.

"Sorry. I was just thinking, from that photo, you might be able to convince people you and Ms. Allen have been seeing each other for a while, and that maybe she wasn't engaged to that secretly gay photographer."

Okay, James couldn't deny that would be useful, if his purpose was truly to keep Chloe's business from going under and maybe…to get to spend some time with Chloe while doing it. And he wanted some time with her. No lying to himself about that anymore. Or he was just nuts right now. Chloe Derangement Syndrome. He'd had it before.

"If anyone asks about Chloe and me, don't deny it," he told Marcy.

Marcy brightened instantly. "That you and Ms. Allen are involved?"

"Right. Tell them that we have been for a while."

Marcy was positively rapturous now. James wouldn't be surprised if Marcy had suggested this whole scheme because he and Chloe would end up in the tabloids some more. Marcy would love every moment of that.

"I want a full briefing on how the riot played in the blogs, the gossip sites…. You know, all that stuff."

"Of course." It was a dream-come-true assignment for Marcy.

"I have to go. Cancel my morning meetings. I'll call you later about what to do with my afternoon schedule."

He had to pitch the plan to Chloe. The one to save her business. She'd do anything to save her business, wouldn't she?

Even pretend to be dating him again?

"He's coming!" Addie whispered furiously to Chloe soon after they unlocked the salon doors that morning, happy to find no rioting brides and only a few tabloid photographers outside.

But now *he* was coming, and there was only one *he,* as far as she was concerned.

"How do I look?" Chloe asked, because she couldn't help herself.

She was still seriously annoyed at how she'd just crawled out of bed, her hair a mess, still wearing her PJs, when he'd seen her yesterday. Every woman had fantasies of how great she'd look the next time a man who broke her heart saw her again, and in all the fantasies, she looked fabulous. He would be shocked at how good she looked, sad he ever lost her, and beg her to take him back. It was a universal female fantasy, and Chloe feared she didn't look good enough for him this time, either.

"You're good. You're very good," Addie said. "Just pinch your cheeks a little bit. You could use some more color. And wet your lips. That's it. You want to look kissable. Very kissable."

"I do?" Chloe wasn't sure she could stand it if he kissed her.

"You're right. It's James. You don't."

Chloe sighed. "Why do you think he's here?"

"I have no idea, but he photographs well, especially in rescue mode. So I think, despite everything else, we should be nice to him."

"Okay. I can do that."

"But not too nice," Addie said. "I don't want him to hurt you again."

"Right. Me, either." She was such a wimp where he was concerned. "Addie, I don't know if I can do this."

"Of course you can. You just had your whole career and your love life land in the toilet, and half the world saw photos and video of it, but you survived. You can handle seeing this man again."

"You're right." He couldn't possibly humiliate her as much as she'd already been humiliated. She had that going for her.

He walked in looking characteristically gorgeous and uncharacteristically unsure of himself. Or maybe he was afraid some disaster might strike at any moment, like the riot he'd been in the midst of the day before. Even Chloe was scared of walking into her own shop right now, so she could understand how he would be, too.

Addie gave her a smile and disappeared, probably just to the other side of the door of the showroom, if Chloe knew her sister. She'd be close if Chloe needed her—and she'd want to hear what James had to say.

Chloe summoned up every bit of courage and confidence she had and put a smile on her face as he slowly walked up to her. Hands stuffed into his pockets, he stood and smiled, just looking at her for a moment.

"Feeling better today, I hope?" he said finally.

She nodded, thinking she really didn't have to speak just yet.

"Good. I was worried about you. You were kind of out of it last night."

"Oh…well…the whole thing was pretty surreal." The mob attack, seeing him again, having him lift her into his arms, carry her up the stairs, put her gently on her bed, kiss her so sweetly, let her fall asleep in his arms….

"I imagine it must have been," he agreed. "I mean, how many people get attacked by angry brides?"

"Even for me, that's weird." She'd always been a different sort of girl, and he knew it, even seemed to enjoy it at times.

"So, things are better today?" he asked. "No mad brides so far?"

"Not this morning."

"Good. I was hoping some good would come of us making the cover of one of the tabloids."

Chloe winced. "I am so sorry about that. I know how much you hate that sort of thing."

He shrugged as if it meant nothing at all to him, when she knew it did. He was a man who liked his privacy, liked peace and quiet in order to be able to concentrate on what he truly enjoyed—his work. He was as much of a workaholic as she was. It had been one thing that worked for them—that devotion and understanding of ambition and long hours.

"I was afraid they were going to hurt you," he said. "And I would never stand by and let someone hurt you, Chloe."

She looked him in the eye then, surprised and terribly pleased.

"I mean…" He shrugged once again and smiled. "I wouldn't just stand by and watch anyone get attacked like that."

"Of course. I knew that. I knew…what you meant," she lied. So all it had been was good manners and being in the right place at the right time?

"So," he said finally. "Marcy says you and I are all over the internet gossip sites today. They liked the photo of us."

"Marcy?" He had a girlfriend looking up everything she could find about him and Chloe on the net?

"My assistant. Brilliant woman. Wharton grad. Well-organized, efficient, careful. She just has a bad habit, embarrassing, really. She loves the tabloids. Please don't tell her I told you so. She'd be horrified that anyone knew."

Chloe laughed, trying to imagine anyone working for him and having a secret tabloid addiction.

"I know. It's ridiculous, but there it is. I guess we all have our secret…weaknesses."

Chloe wanted to hide. Was he talking about her? Did he know that he might be her most guilty secret of all? That her heart still did that crazy little jittery dance just seeing him again? And she was perfectly clearheaded today. She had no excuses.

"So, anyway," he said, "Marcy says the photo of us seems to have stopped the worst of…you know? The stuff about you being cursed in love and your dresses being cursed."

Okay, this was getting worse by the minute. "Well, I appreciate that. That the photograph did that. Thank you."

He nodded, still looking uncomfortable.

What did he have to be uncomfortable about? His life seemed to be going along just fine, no scandals, no business on the verge of collapse, no humiliation.

"So…remember that silly…magazine list I made back when we were together?"

She frowned. "Up-and-Coming Young Businessmen of Manhattan?"

"No, the bachelor list."

"The Single Woman's Guide to Bachelor Hunting in New York?" He'd been outraged by the whole thing, and soon she'd hated it, too. All those women, so pretty, so polished, with money and breeding, seemingly so much more suited to a romance with him than she ever would be.

"Yeah. That." He looked like it truly pained him. "It's

coming out again any day now, and…I'm afraid I'm going to be on it again."

"Oh." Of course he was. He was likely even more successful now than he had been before and still single, as far as she knew.

"So I'm probably going to have some photographers hounding me for a few weeks, like they did the last time."

"You poor thing," she said, hoping her tone didn't come off as too mean or bitter. She really hoped she wasn't bitter.

He shot her a look that said he knew from where she stood, his problems weren't that big or that bad.

"Sorry," she said. "Really. You've been…so nice, and I'm just…sorry."

"Chloe, the thing is…if one photograph of us together was enough to stop women from rioting at your shop… Well, I thought, some more photographs, more gossip, might be enough to turn things around for you and your business."

Her mouth fell open at that, and she feared she heard a tiny whoop of joy from behind the showroom door, where Addie was no doubt hiding. She really couldn't believe it. He'd charged to the rescue like Prince Charming the night before, and now he was offering to try to actually rescue her business?

"You'd do that for me?" she asked, simply unable to stop herself.

He looked uncomfortable once again. "I know how much your business means to you. I know how hard you've worked, what a chance that show at Fashion Week was for you. It's not fair to have it all taken away by…by…"

"Me being stupid enough to fall in love with a guy who has a thing for other guys?" She closed her eyes the second she got the words out. Sometimes her mouth just ran away on her and something like that came out, something so bad and so humiliating…. Now she really, really wanted to disappear.

"We all make mistakes," he said finally, which had her thinking about the end of him and her, that awful argument and then Giselle. Always Giselle.

God, that still hurt. He'd denied it so many times, denied that anything was going on between them, and then, finally, she'd caught them together, and just wanted to die right then and there.

"Look, Chloe, I wouldn't want my mistakes trotted out for all the public to see, and you don't deserve that, either."

She shook her head, staring at the floor, completely unable to look him in the eye. "I don't know what to say."

"It's no big deal," he claimed. "Like I said, I'm going to have photographers following me and taking my picture for a while anyway. Why not give this a try? We go out a couple of times, very public events. People get the idea that we're a couple again. I don't have women hunting me down. At least, not as many women, hopefully. And maybe we can save your business at the same time."

Chloe stood there, thinking that of all the things he could have come here to say, this was the least expected. He was ready to help her? And no matter what he said, he was talking about helping her.

"I can't believe you'd do that for me."

"It just so happens that being linked romantically would work for both of us right now," he insisted.

She wouldn't look like the unluckiest woman in the world in love, not if she had him escorting her around the town. If she were cursed, she wouldn't be able to get anywhere near him.

But she wasn't buying the whole good-for-both-of-us thing. Chloe hadn't seen him in a year and a half. Their breakup had been wretched, at least for her. After catching him with Giselle that day, she'd turned and walked away, returning her engagement ring by messenger, not so much as talking to him again.

He hadn't tried to see her, either, not in all that time. He was a proud, stubborn man, used to getting anything he wanted, to making things work.

Which made her think he had to be up to something. But what?

"James, that's really nice of you," she began. "And I appreciate it, given how badly things ended between us. I just don't think—"

"Chloe!" Addie shouted, bursting through the door and into the showroom, grabbing Chloe by the arm. "Sorry, James. I need her for a minute. I'll have her right back to you."

She dragged Chloe through the door and into the kitchen, then said, "You have to say yes."

"Addie, he's up to something—"

"Maybe—"

"Oh, he is. And we have no idea what that is," Chloe finished.

"Right. We don't. But we also know one other thing. You cannot afford to turn him down. Not now."

Chloe made a face.

"No," Addie insisted. "It is that bad. But yesterday, Prince Charming came to your rescue, looking romantic and absolutely perfect doing it. And thank God someone got a photo of it, and it made the front page of one of those stupid tabloids. Rule No. 1 in PR disasters: you have to change the story. You know, the icky one. He changed the big, icky story."

"Okay, so he changed the story."

"Yeah. Nothing I had thought of would've worked like

that. Nothing I could do. You're not pitiful anymore. You're not cursed. Because a rich, gorgeous man wants you. And now, everyone wants to know who he is. I'm going to make sure they do."

"Addie!" She knew Addie was right, always bowing to Addie's business sense, which was so much stronger than Chloe's. Still, it was hard to hear that right now they needed James.

"Don't worry. No one will know I did it. That awful Bride Blog lady has already told everyone the two of you were engaged once. People are going to figure it out. I'm just going to make sure they do it faster by dropping a few hints into the comments sections of a few gossip sites."

"And then what?"

"Whatever I have to do," Addie claimed. "And he said he's going to be on that bachelor list again. That's perfect. You'll have captured one of New York's most sought-after men. You'll go from Chloe the Cursed to having all the single women in New York envy you. It's perfect. We couldn't buy publicity like this."

Chloe wanted to hide. "But I'll have to see him again."

"Yeah, well, if this doesn't work we may be all selling ourselves in the streets to get operating capital for next month. Which do you want to do?"

"I...I...ahhh!"

"Believe me, if we had time for me to be more sympathetic, I would be," Addie said. "But we're desperate. Now get out there and tell him yes."

She practically shoved Chloe back into the showroom.

James was still standing there, still looking every bit as perfect as before, while she felt bedraggled, rumpled and freakishly cursed.

He frowned at her. "That bad?"

"Hmm?"

"The news Addie had to share with you right away? Was it really that bad?"

"Oh, that." Chloe sighed. She didn't even have the energy to lie to him. "There wasn't any news. She just…she told me I had to tell you yes, that I'd pretend we're back together."

He nodded. "And it sounds that awful? To have to see me again?"

Chloe's eyes came up at that. He sounded oddly vulnerable when he said it, and one thing James Elliott was not was vulnerable. Not ever. She still couldn't figure out what he'd ever seen in her in the first place. They were just such different people. Him, so polished and successful and careful, and her, so…flaky and disorganized and always perched on the brink of insolvency, with a big dream and her whole family depending on her to make things work.

"You don't do anything without a good reason, usually lots of good reasons, and I know you. You could just stay in your office for a few weeks, working practically around the clock on some deal and be perfectly happy, until this whole list thing blows over. You'd probably be happier that way."

"Okay, you're right," he admitted. "There is another reason. I feel guilty."

"Why? Nothing that's happened to me is your fault," she claimed. If she'd gone into her relationship with Bryce too quickly, still stinging from what happened with James, that was on her. Not him.

"No, not about you. About Adam. I talked him into taking over my interest in your business. He did it as a favor to me."

"Oh. Right. And now, if we go under, he's going to take a financial hit from that," Chloe realized. One more person's fate on her conscience. Her whole family and one Adam Landrey, nice investor guy.

"I hate the idea of him losing the money he put into your company. I mean, I hate the idea of you losing everything, too, Chloe. Honestly, I do. None of you deserve that. But with Adam, there's the added guilt that he's in this mess because of me."

"I thought he was loaded. That what he put into my company was nothing to him."

"It was at the time. But times have changed. Lots of people are hurting...." He swore softly. "I have no right to tell you this. Understand? Please, don't ever tell him or anyone else that I told you. But Adam really needs for this to work right now."

"Oh." She felt like a complete failure then, like some kind of plague upon those who loved her and had the supreme misfortune to get involved with her in business. And she couldn't handle ruining one more person's life. Really, she couldn't. If there was a way to stop it, she was going to take it. "Okay, I'll do it."

Chapter Four

"I think this is a really bad idea," Chloe said early that evening, as she stood in front of the big mirrors on the dais in her own showroom, dressed in one of her own bridesmaid's gowns that Connie had just finished altering to fit Chloe.

Chloe could make a gorgeous bridesmaid's gown. None of that awful the-bride-must-be-the-only-beautiful-one-on-her-wedding-day crap for Chloe and anyone serving as a bridesmaid to her brides. So she looked good. Or as good as she could look, considering she wasn't five-ten and twenty pounds underweight, like models were.

But she was seriously freaking out.

Connie knew it, too. She put her dress pins and tape away and said, "I'm going to get Addie." Because in their family, when things got tough, Addie got them through it.

Addie arrived and without any sympathy at all for Chloe, she asked, "Do you want to be bankrupt?"

"No," Chloe insisted.

"Do you want your entire family, all of whom depend on you for work, to be bankrupt along with you, all of us huddled together for warmth, living on the street corner, going through garbage bins to try to find some scraps to eat?"

"No!" Chloe said.

"Then you're going out with that man. You're going to look great, and like you're absolutely thrilled to be by his side at this charity ball, and that's all there is to it!" Addie said, sticking another pin in the gown and catching Chloe's side just a bit, as she tried to make the gown fit perfectly.

"Ouch!" Chloe protested, then tried to explain. "He's up to something! You should have seen his face when I agreed to his little plan. He was so happy—"

"Well, we don't want him looking miserable—"

"But why would he be so happy to go out with me? He must have a reason."

"He does. He said he doesn't want his friend to be eating out of garbage bins with us."

"Adam Landrey isn't going to end up eating out of garbage bins. At worst, four-star restaurants instead of five-star, which means James has to have some other reason for doing this!"

"What if he does? You don't have the luxury of saying no to him, no matter what," Addie insisted.

Chloe's eyes flooded with tears. "Addie, he broke my heart!"

Addie stayed stern. "Don't you dare cry! The makeup artist has already left. If you ruin all her hard work and don't look absolutely radiant in the photographs tonight, I will never forgive you. Do you understand me?"

Chloe sniffled, managing to hold back the tears, but just barely. "I'm scared," she finally whispered.

"We all are. But someone has to be strong. I'm trying to be the strong one now, and once it comes time to actually go out with Prince Charming, you'll be the strong one. Our financial lives depend upon it. I mean, do you really think any of us could function out there in the real world? Working for anyone else?"

"You could." Chloe was sure of it.

"I think I could. Could you or anybody else in our little enterprise?"

"No, I don't think so." They all had their little quirks. Together, they took care of each other, compensated for each other's weaknesses, understood and forgave and moved on. Most people wouldn't, especially not in business.

"Okay, so you have your higher purpose, and you are a brave, strong, wonderfully creative woman, and you're very lucky—"

Chloe sputtered with outrage at the world *lucky.* Addie could be fierce in fighting for the family business, but she went overboard at times.

"I am not lucky," Chloe said.

"Yes, you are. You have a way out. He offered us one. Before he showed up, it looked like we had no chance at all. Now we have one, slim, I admit, but a chance. Don't forget that."

"Okay. You're right. I'm sorry," Chloe said, feeling properly chagrined. Addie always knew what to say, and she was always firmly on Chloe's side. "I just…I can't fall for him again. Addie, I can't—"

"Then don't."

"Easy for you to say. He's never kissed you."

"Don't let him kiss you, either. I mean…those little pecks on the cheek for show in front of the cameras, but that's it. Nothing else."

But he already had. At least Chloe was pretty sure that he had. And that it felt every bit as incredible as it had before, maybe even better. "I just don't want to get my heart broken again. I don't think my heart could take it."

"Look at me," Addie the drill sergeant said. "I know you can do it. Now, let's see what we can do with your hair."

She was still fiddling with Chloe's hair when the little bell at the showroom door tinkled, announcing an arrival. Chloe turned around, braced to see *him* again, only to find a doll-like figure of a woman, her face a splotchy red, eyes brimming over with tears.

Which could only mean… Hysterical Bride.

"Oh, crap," Addie muttered. "I could have sworn Robbie locked that door fifteen minutes ago."

They both pasted on their everything-is-fine faces and walked toward the poor, sad thing. Chloe recognized this one. Denise? Dani? But she knew the dress, a graceful shantung silk due to be finished any day now.

Addie got to the girl, smiled and said, "Hi. What can we do for you?"

"Uhhh…I'm interrupting something."

"No, no, Chloe is all ready. She's wearing one of her own gowns. Doesn't she look great?"

The teary bride nodded slowly, then asked Chloe, "You're going out?"

Chloe nodded.

"Really? I just thought…well…it just sounded like…"

Like Chloe wouldn't be caught dead out in public right now? Yeah. She knew.

"She's going to the big charity ball at the Metropolitan Museum tonight," Addie bragged.

"Oh," the little bride said.

And if I can do this, you can walk down the aisle in one of my dresses, Chloe thought.

"Well, I just…I'm Daniella Santini. I ordered a dress a while back—"

"Of course. A fitted champagne-colored bodice with a full ballerina skirt in shantung silk. I bet you're so excited." Chloe put on her calmest, most reassuring, dealing-with-Hysterical-Brides smile. "Your big day is so close."

"I am." Daniella's bottom lip quivered and she looked a little guilty. "I'm sorry. It's just that…the dress isn't going to work!"

"Of course it will. It's going to be perfect," Chloe claimed. "Remember how you looked in the sample? So perfect with your complexion."

Not at the moment, because poor Daniella was all splotchy, but as long as she didn't bawl on her wedding day, she'd be gorgeous. Chloe whispered urgently to Addie to go get Robbie. He was the best with Hysterical Brides.

"I thought it was what I wanted," Daniella admitted. "But…well…it's just not. And I came to tell you I don't want the dress."

"Did you and your fiancé have a fight? Daniella, I can't tell you how many couples fight in the days leading up to their weddings—"

"No, it's not that. Mark is…well, he's a beautiful dresser, a better one than I am, and he's fussy about his clothes and has a really good eye for color. He loves Broadway musicals and has no interest at all in sports. Not that it means anything, really. I mean, he loves me. I know he does."

"I'm sure he does," Chloe claimed, getting a bad feeling about this.

"But my great-aunt Margene, who's helping pay for the wedding… She's always had some reservations about Mark. I told her she was being ridiculous but she met the best man yesterday, and Tom is absolutely gorgeous." Daniella sobbed the last part.

Gotta watch those gorgeous best men.

"He and Mark have been best friends forever, room-mates in college, and after that thing with your...your... you know what I mean!" she cried. "My aunt thinks Mark likes men! She says I'd be crazy to get married in a gown designed by you. That it would be tempting fate. I'm sorry. I just can't do it. Someone told me you were giving people their money back for dresses?"

Chloe's humiliation, feeling as fresh as if it had just hap-pened minutes ago, washed over her anew, as she heard the little bell over the front door again.

Of course James chose that moment to walk into the shop, smiling with the confidence, grace and take-charge attitude that seemed to carry him throughout every mo-ment of his life.

"I'm sorry." He came to Chloe's side, slid an arm around her waist and kissed her softly on the cheek, like a man with every right to do so, and then said, "Am I interrupt-ing?"

Daniella just stared at him.

Chloe stepped in. "Daniella, this is my...friend James Elliott. James, this is Daniella Santini, who's getting mar-ried soon in one of my gowns."

"I'm sure you'll be perfect in one of Chloe's gowns." James took Daniella's hand, bent over it and kissed it in a way that didn't look silly at all. That looked as natural and charming as could be and rendered Daniella momentarily speechless.

She looked from James to Chloe, then back to James again, no doubt wondering what in the world this beauti-ful, polished, important-looking man was doing looking down at Chloe like she was the only woman in the world. Chloe sincerely hoped Daniella's fiancé looked at her in just that way.

The look seemed to work for a moment, and then it just didn't anymore.

Daniella started to stammer, clearly trying to get rid of James, who played dumb and stayed where he was. Then Addie and Robbie showed up.

Daniella finally blurted out, "I'm afraid my fiancé's gay!"

Chloe felt like a balloon that had just sprung a giant leak. If she could just deflate to the point where she disappeared, that would be great.

"Oh, honey." Robbie, who was gay himself, jumped in and tried to save the day. "I remember your fiancé. The man knows how to dress and knows his art and modern theater. But I know a gay man when I see one, and believe me, he's as straight as they come. Gorgeous, but straight."

Daniella sniffled a bit, then asked, "Really? You're sure?"

"I'm sure." Robbie patted her shoulder and handed her a tissue.

Daintily, she wiped her tears away. "But, did you know...that other man...Chloe's other man... Did you know he was gay?"

Chloe gave a little yelp.

"You know," James said, coming to her rescue. His smile hadn't diminished one bit. If anything, it radiated with even more confidence and charm, as he pulled Chloe even closer and told Daniella, "You can't believe everything you read."

Daniella looked truly bewildered, but she'd stopped crying, at least. "Uh...you mean...the two of you are... together?"

Chloe felt herself smiling, hopefully not one of those kill-me-now smiles.

"Does she look like a woman who's devastated because she just found out her fiancé is gay?" James asked.

"Well...no," Daniella admitted. "I guess not. It's just... I—I can't have anything like that happen to me. I'd just die if it did."

Or wish you could, Chloe thought.

"You are going to be so beautiful in the gown Chloe made for you that no man would ever dream of leaving you for any reason," James claimed.

And after a few more minutes of reassurance, Daniella seemed to believe it. She dabbed at her eyes once again, told James how nice it was to meet him and said she'd be in to pick up her gown next Wednesday. Crisis averted, at least with poor Daniella.

Chloe still had James to deal with.

He eased away from her as Daniella left, and the arm that had been around her waist, anchoring her to him, dropped to his side. He shot Robbie a pointed look that said without a word, *Go away now.*

"We'll just...leave you two alone. Have a great date," Robbie said, giving Chloe a little kiss on the cheek and whispering, "You can do this."

He and Addie walked out of the room, leaving Chloe all alone with James.

"Well," she said, "that was good timing."

He nodded. "How many Hysterical Brides have you had today?"

"Daniella was the first," she admitted.

"Good. This is going to work, you know?" He stood back and looked her over from head to toe, taking in the simple, shimmery silk crepe gown in a barely pink color called blush, and finally said, "You're lovely."

"Thank you."

"Will I do? Or do you want to dress me?"

Chloe knew Addie had called his assistant—the previously mentioned Marcy, who was indeed very excited about simply talking to a relative of Chloe-from-the-tabloids fame—to give James some direction on what color shirt and tie to wear. The object, after all, was for the two of them to look great in the photos or video of them going into the event.

No doubt about it, the man knew how to dress. His suits were impeccably cut and fit like a dream, but he seldom ventured from the same color palette—white dress shirt, dark-colored tie to match his dark-colored suit of the day, which he was in now.

Chloe studied him, trying to look with the eye of a designer and not a woman at his near-perfect body. She took a breath, feeling tired and overwhelmed at the moment. It really wasn't fair that he still looked every bit as good as ever.

"Robbie pulled a couple of shirts and ties for you. Nothing too threatening, I promise. Just a shirt the same shade as my gown." She would not mention the words *blush* or *pink* when dressing a man.

"I am not threatened in the least by colors. At least not those colors," he said, looking at the rack of shirts in the corner. "They're all white. Or nearly white. I'm already wearing white."

"Then you shouldn't be afraid of any of these shirts. Just think of them as white. And you can keep your tie, if you want."

"You still think I'm color-blind, don't you?" he asked, loosening the tie and then pulling it off, shrugging off the suit jacket, as well.

"You can afford to have at least one flaw," she said, as he started unbuttoning his shirt right there in front of her.

No big deal. At least it shouldn't be. She'd seen him

without his shirt. Many times. It was just…she really didn't need to see him calmly, methodically undressing right now, taking her back to that first night they'd met.

She'd been coordinating a charity fashion show, and her model groom was missing. She'd hired him for the show based on a headshot, so she knew his face. When she'd walked out the back door and seen a man she thought was him, rushing down the street like he was late, Chloe had grabbed him. Before he could protest, she'd dragged him inside, scolding him all the way and telling him to get out of his clothes, that the show was starting.

She'd literally been undressing him herself—the tie gone, the shirt buttons in progress—when she'd noticed his grin, so dazzling, so potent and so clearly heterosexual and interested. *In her.* Chloe had been around a lot of male models, and this was not the way they looked at her.

Her hands froze on his chest, and she made a slow study of him, the dark hair, dark eyes, sexy grin, the very expensive cut of his suit, the sleek build that hid an unexpectedly muscular chest, the way he just stood there, a model of cooperation, waiting to see what she would do.

Three people shouted questions at her. The show was literally about to start. She answered them all, made decisions, shouted orders, and all the while he just stood there, waiting, making it nearly impossible for her to so much as drag her eyes away from him.

Finally, she said, "You're not my missing model, are you?"

He shook his head, never taking his eyes off her, a look of pure appreciation on his face.

"Then why didn't you say so? Why did you let me drag you in here and start taking your clothes off?" she asked, only then realizing she was still touching him. She jerked her hands away, like she'd had them on a hot stove. "And I swear, if you say something stupid and utterly predictable, like, 'I never refuse when a woman grabs me and tells me to take my clothes off,' don't bother. I don't have time."

He shrugged, still grinning. "I was just trying to be helpful. You need a man? Can I help?"

"I...I...you're not a model?"

"No."

But he did look the part and was willing. She frowned, studied him again. "What size suit do you wear?"

He laughed out loud. "Thirty-eight long."

"No. The tux we brought wouldn't fit. Although the suit you have on is not bad." Italian silk, and it fit him impeccably. This man did not buy off-the-rack. "Can you walk?"

"Since I was eight months old, I'm told."

Chloe nodded. "Overachiever, were you?"

"Right from the start," he bragged.

"Janie, come over here and let me see him walk with you," she called out to one of her brides, then as they waited for the female model to arrive, looked back to him. "I just need you to walk down the runway with her. On, off, over in a moment. Will you do it?"

"If you'll have dinner with me," he shot back.

Chloe gaped at him. "You can't be serious."

"I'm almost always serious. Women seem to think that's a fault."

Chloe had trouble believing women found fault with him at all. Still, the show really was starting any moment. "Look around. You're in a room full of models, absolutely gorgeous women, and you want to go out with me?"

"If you'll notice, I haven't taken my eyes off you since the moment you grabbed me on the street and dragged me in here. I haven't wanted to look at anyone else."

Chloe thought he was nuts. "Why?"

"I think you're interesting. And adorable. And different than the women I normally date—"

"Don't tell me. You normally date the models?"

He shrugged easily, as if it didn't matter at all. "I think you'll find I'm very clear in what I want and very good at getting it. I'm also known to have excellent negotiation skills. I want you to go out with me, and I'm willing to walk anywhere you want to make that happen. Do we have a deal?"

"Unbelievable!" Chloe began, ready to bawl him out for daring take advantage of a crisis in her show to bribe her into going out with him.

But right then, her missing model had shown up. She'd turned all her attention into getting him out of what he was wearing and into the tux.

She'd stood in her place just behind the curtain, coordinating the show, the last person who saw the models before they walked out onto the runway, making sure they were perfect. When it was over, James had still been standing there in the background, watching her and grinning that sexy, tempting grin of his, looking even more handsome and appealing than the missing model she'd mistaken him for.

And she'd agreed to go out with him.

Chloe finally dragged herself back to the present. He'd undone the last button on his shirt and stood there with a strip of skin showing between the sides of the open shirt, taut, tanned, perfect skin, a sprinkling of hair on his chest, fine ripples of muscles on his firm, flat abdomen.

"You're thinking of the first night we met," he said.

She didn't even try to argue. No way she could have pulled off a denial. All the old feelings were too close to the surface, the scene too familiar.

"I was interested from the moment you grabbed me and

told me to take my clothes off. What man wouldn't have been?" He shrugged easily, grinned that same potent grin. "But what really got me was that by the time I'd stood there and watched you work, pull that show together in this crazy frenzy of intensity, passion, sheer joy...I couldn't take my eyes off you. It's like you bewitched me on the spot."

"Don't say that. Don't do that."

"It's true, Chloe." He got his cuffs undone, one by one, and then shrugged out of the shirt, never taking his eyes off her the whole time.

Maybe she was just weak, she decided.

Weak and stupid.

She'd just never made good decisions about men. She tried. She really did. Tried to be careful and smart and take her time. She really didn't want to be hurt, to have her heart broken. What woman did? It was like she lacked some vital strand of DNA. The part that helped women choose a good man, one that would stay. One that knew how to love. One that had an attention span that lasted longer than it took for him to get a woman into bed.

If a woman couldn't be trusted to exercise common sense in choosing a man, then she had no business with any man. No matter how good James Elliott looked without his shirt.

"You look like you're about to be sick," he said, seeming concerned.

"Just coming to some decisions," she said, walking over to the rack of shirts. She had to get him dressed again, fast, before she did something stupid.

Like grab him and kiss him silly.

"So, what did you decide?" he asked, taking the shirt from her.

"That I'm done with men," she said.

He frowned, pausing once he'd gotten the shirt on but

not buttoned yet. "Going to start playing for the other team?"

"What?" She didn't play any kind of sports, but then realized he wasn't talking about sporting teams. "No, I'm not…switching teams. Although, I guess that was one possible story we could have tried. That Bryce was actually gay, and I was a lesbian, and we were just seeing each other to cover up the fact that we were both gay. We didn't think of that. I wonder if straight women would have a problem buying a wedding dress from a designer who was a lesbian?"

James looked at her like she'd lost her mind. "I have no idea."

She shrugged. "You've got to admit, it's better than buying a wedding dress from someone who doesn't believe in love."

"You believe in the tooth fairy, the Easter bunny and Little Mermaid, Chloe. Of course you believe in love."

Her mouth had run away with her once again, or maybe it was that lack of a certain decision-making gene. She admitted softly, "I don't think I do."

He came closer, too close, took her by the arms and just waited there, right in front of her, until she looked up at him, hoping he couldn't see just how badly her heart had been broken, hoping, and failing badly, she feared. He took her face in one of his hands, rubbed his thumb back and forth across her chin like he needed to know if her skin still felt the same to him.

"He really hurt you. I'm sorry, Chloe."

She was outraged at first, then so very sad and then mad all over again, and she just had to save herself, at least this time.

Did he realize that he'd hurt her ten times worse than Bryce ever could have?

Chloe was still thinking of what to say to him when she saw a flash of light behind her. Before she could turn around to see what it was, James took her firmly in his arms this time, his head bending down low to hers like he was going to kiss her any minute.

Chapter Five

"Don't look," he said, his lips practically on hers. "It's probably just a photographer."

"Staking out my showroom again! I thought they'd at least given up on that for the day. And Addie tipped a few of them off that we were going to the benefit. Why aren't they there, waiting for us?"

"Maybe one of them wanted something no one else would have. Isn't that always their goal? To see the thing no one else sees?"

"And he sees us having a fight—"

"No, he's going to see us make up."

Chloe practically growled, she was so mad.

James laughed. "It's a moment, Chloe. We just need to give him a moment that looks really good."

And with that, he slipped one of the skinny, slinky straps of her dress off one of her shoulders and dipped his head down low, like he was nibbling on her shoulder, her neck.

He didn't.

Not really.

But he got close enough that she knew with everything in her that his mouth was less than a half an inch away from her skin. His warm breath skimmed over her. She sucked in a breath and tried not to feel…anything.

Like that had any shot of working.

God must just hate her, Chloe decided. First, he didn't give her that not-stupid-around-men gene, and now she was supposed to stand here with James all but nibbling on her neck and not feel anything? Not do anything to give herself away?

It was too much to expect from any mortal woman.

"Remember, you're supposed to at least look like you like this." James moved over to the other shoulder and took down that strap with his teeth.

She grabbed at the bodice of her dress before it could fall down. "I'm not willing to show that much skin, even if it would save my company."

He laughed, his nose skimming along her collarbone, into that little hollow at the base of her neck. He spent a long moment there, and then worked his way up from her chin, along her jaw and finally stopped just shy of her ear.

Every nerve ending in her traitorous body was on high alert, silently begging him to touch her, really touch her. She feared she whimpered aloud.

"Chloe, you're acting like a statue. Put your hands on my shoulders."

"I'll drop my dress. There's nothing left to hold it up."

"Don't worry." He pressed his body firmly against hers, his chest now leaving nowhere for her dress to go. "I've got it."

She closed her eyes, her dress safely in place, but her breasts now nestled firmly against the wall of his chest.

This close, his body felt even better than before. She willed her hands to his shoulders.

"That wasn't so hard, was it?" he asked.

She slid one hand to the side of his face, the other into his hair and gave it a hard tug.

He laughed, the rat, and took a little nibble of her neck for real. "You want to play nice or not?"

"Nice, please," she said, still feeling those warm, soft lips on her neck, her nerve endings practically dancing with joy, the sensation shooting all the way down her spine.

"Okay. We'll play nice." He skimmed his nose up and down the side of her neck, inhaling deeply.

That was not her idea of nice. "James—"

"Just another moment. We want to make sure the guy gets a good shot."

"He got the shot already! He got dozens of shots," she said, pushing him away. "I just broke my engagement to a secretly bisexual photographer. I know how long it takes to get a dozen good shots off."

She was distracted by her dress nearly falling down, catching it just in time before the stupid photographer really got a shot.

"You were really engaged to a guy who was secretly bisexual?" James asked, either in disbelief or astonishment.

"I don't know what he actually was. I don't know if anything he ever said to me was true. He could just be one more man who lied about who he was sleeping with, claiming that he wasn't sleeping with anybody but me. I don't know. Men should come with those little GPS microchips you can have injected into your dog, so you can check at any moment and know where they are. It would make things so much simpler for women and stop so much lying."

James just looked at her. "I didn't go near another woman in the time we were together—"

"That's certainly one way to put it—"

"Chloe, I swear to you—"

"I guess, in your mind, you didn't go near any of those women. They all came chasing after you."

And she knew that was unfair. Because women did chase him. She'd watched it happen again and again. Women wanted him. Some of them weren't shy about that, even with her standing next to him. It had amused her at first because she'd had him. Or at least, she thought she had him. For a while. Eventually the whole thing had become infuriating and then simply impossible.

He let her have her say, waiting with a grim kind of patience, and then said, "We're going to have to talk about this, Chloe. You don't believe me right now. I know that, but—"

"I don't believe anything any man has to say right now! I mean, would you, if you were me?"

"All right. I guess not," he admitted.

She glared at him. "In fact, now that I think about it, that's exactly what Bryce said. That he'd never been unfaithful to me. He just forgot to mention that his idea of being unfaithful involved being with another woman. He claimed he hadn't done that. He just needed a man every now and then!"

"Oh," James said.

"Yes, oh! Now you know everything. I hope you're satisfied—"

"Hey!" Addie opened the showroom door and yelled at them. "You're not supposed to be fighting, remember? You're supposed to be happy. Chloe, I don't care if it kills you. Be nice to him."

And then she disappeared back into the kitchen.

Chloe stopped yelling, stopped doing everything except glaring at him. He knew every humiliating secret now. There were none left. Except the awful possibility that she wouldn't have fallen for Bryce in the first place if she hadn't been still reeling from her breakup with James.

Please, God, let her keep that one secret, at least.

"I'm sorry," she said finally, utterly defeated and still facing an entire evening with him.

"Me, too," he said.

"This is really hard."

He nodded, then smiled softly, sweetly, showing her his most charming self. "I'll behave. I'll be so good, you'll have trouble believing I'm me."

So if she asked him not to really touch her, not to hold her, not to kiss her, he wouldn't? Unless there was a camera in their faces? Or he'd do it, but not mean it? Was he capable of kissing a woman and not making her turn to mush inside? She couldn't ask because then he'd know her awful secret.

"Come on," he said. "Let's go save your dream."

To fool everyone into thinking they were in love. That no one's heart was broken and that little girls who for their whole lives had imagined they'd one day walk down the aisle to their very own Prince Charming were safe in entrusting part of their dreams to Chloe and one of her gowns.

She had to admit, he was a perfect gentleman from that moment on, as attentive and solicitous as could be when in the public eye, and quietly helpful and considerate— nothing more—when they were alone in the back of the limousine going to the party.

When they arrived at the museum, she took his hand and let him help her out of the limo, then stood there beside him, smiling like she absolutely adored him as they posed together for the cameras.

Inside the party, populated by the minor celebrities, politicians, New York socialites and rich financiers he'd come to court, she tried to feel like she belonged, dressed in silk and bits of vintage jewelry, with a beautiful, rich, powerful man at her side.

She danced with him, so close she breathed in the scent of him with every breath she took. She could feel all those lovely muscles of his pressed up against her, hear people whispering about them, feel them watching, but no one said anything horrible to her face.

He brought her fancy chocolates and champagne—just enough to try to help relax her a bit, no more—and introduced her to dozens of people. All the while he smiled broadly, a hand draped casually at her back, like he couldn't stand for her to stray from his side.

It was exhausting, and after an hour of mingling among the rich and fashionable, he escorted her back to the limo for the drive home.

She eased over as far to the other side of the limousine as possible, liking him a little too much at the moment. He sat on his side, looking like he was up to something but not making any move toward her.

"You're very good at this," she said.

"You make that sound like a bad thing, Chloe."

She frowned. "And I still think you're up to something."

"All I was thinking was that those shoes look great, but they're probably killing your feet. I could do something about that."

"See? There you go. Definitely up to something," she complained.

He held his hands up in mock surrender. "You're perfectly free to stay way over there, and I'll stay here. I think

even you have to admit I've been a model of good behavior
so far. Don't want to ruin that this late in the date. I was
just offering to help. That's all."

"You're being too helpful."

"Maybe you're just too suspicious," he countered. "Did
you ever think of that?"

"Of course I'm suspicious. All women should be suspicious around men. It should be automatic behavior, taught
from birth. Trust no man. Especially the ones who seem
nice."

"Okay, I'll work harder to find the perfect balance between being nice but not too nice. Anything else?"

She sighed. Her feet were killing her. She'd been thinking of slipping off her high heels before he said anything
about her feet. She got so tired sometimes, trying to keep
everything going, make things work for everyone else, and
it seemed like no one took care of her. Ever.

Her family looked out for her, and they were definitely
on her side, ready with advice and encouragement. But
care was a different thing. There were times when she
so wanted someone to take care of her for just a few moments in time. Little pampering, indulgent things. And
then James did the most awful thing, a devious, disarm-
ing thing.

He reached over and took her hand in his.

Just held it in his big warm one.

Nothing else.

Like he'd read her mind once again and knew she was
so tired, so sad, so alone.

He was a magic man, she'd decided when she first met
him. There was some mystical quality to him that let him
see right inside of her, that left her with no defenses against
him, left her thinking he was perfect and put on this earth
just for her. His hand felt like a lifeline, like strength and

safety and an unlimited supply of support and kindness. How was a woman supposed to resist that? Especially when her life was falling apart.

"Slip your shoes off," he whispered through the darkness of the limousine, his voice like a spell.

It was what she wanted. She toed off her sandals and eased sideways, angling her body toward his so she could lean her side against the back of the seat. Then she drew her legs up and let him pull her bare feet onto his thigh.

Chloe closed her eyes and just let herself feel. He did nothing but smooth his hands slowly from her right heel to her toes at first, warming her foot with his hands. And then he stroked softly with his thumbs, finding little sore muscles and trying to smooth them out.

She clamped her lips shut so she wouldn't groan out loud. Because it felt so good. Kind, caring and sexy as could be, an incredibly potent combination.

"You took lessons in that, didn't you?" she asked finally.

He laughed softly, started to say something, then caught himself and gave her a small, sad smile.

Not lessons.

Okay, private lessons, maybe.

From a woman.

Not Chloe. In his post-Chloe period, hopefully, not during-Chloe. But they weren't going to talk about that.

She made the mistake of closing her eyes, as if that would stop her from thinking about exactly who had taught him to touch a woman this way, and it actually worked, kind of. Because closing down one of the five senses always intensified the workings of the others, and she seemed to feel what he was doing that much more intensely.

"Someone once told me you can get a woman to do

practically anything you want with a good foot massage," he said finally.

"She was right," Chloe said, trying not to glare at him as she said it.

He put her foot down and then said, "Give me the other one."

And she did it, because he asked, and because it just felt so good.

She could have those hands all over her whole body, she knew. He could be very kind, very patient when he wanted to be, always a very attentive lover. He could make her purr like a satisfied kitten.

And then where would she be?

Crazy about another man who'd break her heart in the end.

"It's just too hard sometimes, you know?" she whispered.

"Life?"

She nodded.

"Sometimes," he agreed softly. "And sometimes, it gets better."

"You really believe that?"

"I do, Chloe."

"Well, I'm not sure I do."

"You're just tired, and you've had some tough times lately. That's all," he said, those firm, warm hands of his squeezing slowly down the sole of her foot.

If her feet could talk, they'd be singing, it felt so good. It was getting harder and harder to remember why she had to stay away from him.

He went on for a glorious eternity, and when he finally stopped and let one hand rest on top of her left foot, the other slid ever so slowly up her leg, just to the point above her ankle, cupping that muscle and squeezing ever so slightly, his thumb moving lazily back and forth against the side of her leg, her whole body singing the please-touch-me song.

She was more relaxed than she'd been in weeks, felt a little pampered and more than a little turned on. Those magic hands of his could slide up her legs, up her dress, and soon he'd have her laid out flat on the seat with him on top of her.

Just like that.

And she was a fool.

"So what do you really want?" she asked, lying limp against the back of the seat, her feet still in his lap, his hands on her but still now.

"I already told you."

"You lied," she insisted, but without heat. "What's in this for you?"

"Assuaging my guilt over bringing you and Adam Landrey together."

"What else?"

"You just can't believe I would simply want to help anyone?"

"No. Not that," she said truthfully. "Just that you're... so focused, so driven, you hardly have time to think about anyone else. You're always five steps ahead of everyone—"

"So I'm too self-centered to help you and Adam?"

"I didn't say that. I'm just trying to understand."

The limousine slowed down, then stopped. Chloe glanced out the tinted window. She was home.

James got out. He must have told the driver to stay put, because he was the one who opened Chloe's door, her shoes in his hand.

"Want to walk?" he asked. "Or should we go for the Prince Charming, scoop-her-up-and-carry-her-inside treatment again? It did work really well in the first photos, I thought."

"I can walk," she insisted.

So he eased down onto his heels, took one foot in his hand and carefully slipped one sandal on, then the other, then took her hand and helped her out of the limousine.

He walked her to the door, took her keys from her hand and unlocked it, then gave her the keys back and gathered her in his arms. She stiffened, not expecting that, trying to hold herself just a little bit away from him and that alluring heat of his, the strength, the way he smelled.

She must be the strongest woman alive to resist him, she decided.

He leaned his head down to hers, his lips right at the side of her mouth. But he didn't kiss her, just whispered, "We don't know who might still be watching."

And then stayed there, perfectly still, his arms wound around her in a way that had to look possessive, like the perfect way to end a perfect date, just shy of being invited to come upstairs.

She let herself snuggle against him just a bit, easing just a little closer, her senses enveloped just a tad more completely in him. All she had to do was ease her mouth a fraction of an inch to the right, and he'd be kissing her, devouring her, she suspected. Or she'd be devouring him.

Two flights of stairs, down one hall, inside one door, and they could be in her room, in her bed. She shivered, thinking of them there, the way it had been so many times.

"I remember everything about what it was like to be with you," he whispered, sounding like a man who ached for her, and yet not moving one tiny millimeter closer, the discipline as astonishing as it was frustrating.

She finally broke the spell, not strongly enough to pull away from him but to let her head fall to his shoulder, to nestle into that wonderful hollow between his shoulder and his neck.

He breathed deeply, slowly, easing her body more firmly against his, wrapping her more tightly in his arms, like he was a man who'd stand between her and the entire world, if necessary.

And that's really what he was doing at the moment.

"You're going to have to tell me to leave," he said finally, his voice low and sexy, like he was as reluctant to go as she was to have him go.

The only problem was, she was even more scared to have him stay.

"I am an absolute mess right now," she said.

He grinned, laughed just a bit. She could feel the sound rumbling through his chest. "You're always kind of a mess, Chloe. But you're so much more than that. You always have been. And you never understood how appealing that could be."

"You can't be telling me that you've missed me," she insisted.

He eased back and nudged her head up, so he could look her in the eye. "I have missed you. Terribly. Tell me you've missed me, too."

Silly tears glistened in her eyes, coming on in a rush. "I've missed you, and I've been furious at you. I've cursed you and the day you were born, your mother, your father, every ancestor you ever had and now that damned woman who taught you to rub my feet that way! I've cried and cried and cried over you. I had a giant bonfire in the backyard and burned everything you ever gave me—"

"Okay, that's a little scary, Chloe—"

"I've done everything I could think of to get over you, to forget all about you, and now you come waltzing back into my life at the absolute worst possible time, looking every bit as gorgeous as before and being impossibly nice and saying you just want to help, and I can't say no to that help—"

"Good," he said.

"I can't say no, but I want to. I want desperately to just say no and tell you to go away because…because…"

"Yes? Because…why?"

She backed up until she couldn't anymore, her back against the shop door. Then she nearly yelled, "You know why!"

"Tell me," he insisted, following her until he was right up against her again. "I need to hear it, Chloe. Tell me. Because you—"

"Ahhh!" Chloe yelled as she nearly fell backward into the shop as the door behind her gave way. James nearly fell on top of her. He caught himself with one hand on the doorframe, caught her with his other hand and managed to keep them both on their feet, barely.

"What is the matter with you two?" Addie stood there holding the door open, glaring at them both. "You can't spend a few hours together without fighting? You're supposed to be crazy in love, remember? Prince Charming and that whole stupid fairy-tale courtship thing? And here you are yelling at each other before you can even get inside the shop!"

"Sorry," James said.

"You're never going to make this work at this rate! We'll fail miserably, and then we'll all end up living on the streets, begging for loose change and wrapping ourselves up in very expensive silk wedding gowns for warmth, because no one will want to buy them. Because we're all cursed! We can't even pull off a decent illusion of love for two stupid hours!"

"Addie, honey. It's okay. Go back to bed," Chloe said.

"No," she insisted. "Not until he's gone."

"Okay. I'll go," James said, giving Chloe one long, probing look.

He likely wanted to pin her to the wall and torture her until he got her to admit she needed another chance with him. He had to know how close he'd come to getting her to do just that.

But Addie could be scary when she was mad or scared herself, and James was a patient man, a wickedly patient one when it suited him. All as a means to getting what he wanted eventually. That was another truly scary thing about him—how he almost always got what he wanted in the end.

He leaned in, the perfect gentleman once again, kissed Chloe softly on the cheek, whispered, "Good night," and left.

Chloe collapsed on the showroom floor and buried her head in her hands, Addie fussing and wanting to know what was wrong. But Chloe couldn't even get the words out.

He wants me back.

Chapter Six

James was whistling as he approached the newsstand the next morning and Vince presented him with a tabloid with a photo of him and Chloe on the front page. Shot through the windows of her darkened shop, it was a shadowy impression of the two of them in an embrace, looking downright erotic as he nibbled on her neck.

Damn.

He got a little hot just looking at it, and he knew there hadn't been that much to the whole interlude. He hadn't actually touched her delectable neck.

"Looks like she's a lot more than your ex. You've been holdin' out on me," Vince said.

James shook his head. "I haven't."

"The hell you say," Vince insisted. "Come on. It's me. Was she really engaged to that photographer guy? And if she wasn't, what was that big fight on the runway about?"

"Vince, just out of curiosity, how much of the stuff do you think they print in these tabloids you sell is true?"

Vince shrugged. "I don't know. How much of the stuff do you think that's in the regular newspapers is true?"

"Okay, you've got me there."

James put the *Wall Street Journal* and his money down on the counter.

"You don't even want copies of the tabloids you're in today?"

"Nope." No doubt Marcy would have copies waiting. He couldn't deprive her of the pleasure of sharing all the news with him.

He was still whistling when he walked into the office. His secretary, his secretary's secretary and Marcy all stared at him like he'd lost his mind.

"What?" he asked finally.

"We thought you wouldn't be happy today, because of the photographs," Marcy said. "You have seen the photographs, haven't you?"

"Yes, I've seen the photographs."

Still, they stared.

"You just usually hate being photographed and showing up in the paper. Especially the tabloids," Marcy said.

"Oh, right. Yes. Awful, isn't it?" He tried, knowing even as he did that he wasn't selling it the way he should. He couldn't even pretend this morning.

Now they really looked at him like he'd lost his mind. *Oh, well.*

"Marcy, in here. Now," he said, pointing to his office. That was a little more like it, at least. He always started his day by ordering Marcy around.

She practically ran into the office, a little folder clutched to her chest, closed the door behind him and then stood behind his desk and to his right side.

"I have everything ready for you to review," she said, putting the folder down in front of him and opening it to a photo of him and Chloe arriving at the benefit. "This is the sort of shot used most frequently, correctly identifying you and Ms. Allen, mentioning that you had been involved previously. Many of them noted the prior engagement, and they all mentioned the runway brawl, but usually in questioning whether previous stories about it were true."

"Excellent," James said.

"Yes, it is. And then we have…this…particular photo…."

The shadowy shot of them in each other's arms in her shop.

He grinned, couldn't help it.

Marcy stared at him, waited and waited. He wasn't talking.

"This…uhhh," she finally continued, "one of the tabloids had this, claiming it's you and Ms. Allen, although it's hard to tell for sure. I wasn't sure if I should deny that it's the two of you or…"

"This is like a dream come true to you, isn't it?" he asked. "A front-row seat to front-page tabloid news?"

"I'm just trying to be prepared," Marcy argued. "The shot is out there, and if someone asks me about it, I have to know what to say."

"You don't have to say anything," James told her.

She pouted a bit, but went on to the various Chloe news items on the internet gossip sites, from "Chloe doesn't waste any time moving on" to "Chloe doesn't look like a woman with a broken heart."

"This one notes that Chloe may have already captured one of New York's most eligible, and that the list is coming out any day now."

"I can live with that."

"And then there's the Bride Blog lady."

James groaned. "What is wrong with this woman?"

"I think she hates Chloe. She's so mean. This morning

she says that Chloe's ex, Bryce Gorman, is being treated by the best plastic surgeon in the city but is likely to be scarred for life, that his boyfriend is either waiting tearfully by Bryce's side, pleading with Eloise to take him back or heavily medicated in a psychiatric ward in upstate New York, his life ruined. All while Chloe goes blithely on with her life, picking up where she left off with you, because she needs you for your money once again."

So, she was supposedly using him for his money? Something like that was always in the back of his mind when he was with a woman, but not Chloe. Maybe ninety-five percent of the time he was sure Chloe wasn't like that, and the rest of the time, he was just plain mad about the whole question of women, money and trust.

"This is just trash, Marcy. Don't believe a word of it," he said, then went to work.

Addie called James's office first thing the morning after Chloe's outing to the Met, ready to give him a piece of her mind, but was told quite snottily that he was in a meeting and could not be disturbed. It was a full hour before the phone rang again, caller ID telling her the call was coming from James's office.

"You rat! What did you do to her last night?" she said, not even bothering with "hello." They were long past pleasantries.

But it turned out it wasn't even him, just a woman who said she was his assistant, Marcy. She promised to messenger over the press clippings and internet postings of the day about Chloe and James, showing the initial success of their quest to prove Chloe was not cursed in love.

Then she started talking about how happy James was that morning, smiling—whistling even—despite that steamy photo of him and Chloe in the shop, where it looked like he was undressing her with his teeth.

"Oh, that rat!" Addie said. "He needs to understand that they are most certainly not back together. They're just pretending. That's it. She doesn't want him back for real, and he can't have her. He has to know that, if he has a functioning brain cell in his body."

"Oh, well—"

And then Addie got the worst feeling. "He's up to something, isn't he? He's got some hidden agenda with her, and when I get my hands on him, I am going to kill him!"

"I don't think he's up to anything. I mean…you wouldn't really hurt him, would you? Because he's a brilliant man. A financial genius and…a little different, but he's not evil. Besides, I don't think I've ever seen him really care that much about a woman. They come. They go. It doesn't really matter to him. Another one will come along sooner or later. They always do—"

The line went dead, suddenly nothing but silence, then a dial tone.

That was odd.

Suddenly, Addie had a bad feeling about the whole conversation.

James lunged for the phone, reaching around Marcy to slam his finger down on the disconnect button.

Marcy gave a little yelp, hung up the phone and slowly turned to face him.

"Another woman will come along? They always do?" he yelled. "Did you really just say that?"

She nodded shakily.

"What the hell did you just do, Marcy?"

"I'm sorry. I am so sorry. I was trying to help—"

"Help? By telling Chloe I don't give a damn about her, much less any woman?"

"No, no, no. It wasn't Chloe!" she cried.

"Oh, thank God," he said.

"It was her assistant, Addie."

James winced. "Addie's not just one of her assistants. She's her half sister. And she hates me! Absolutely hates me."

"She did say something about wanting to kill you." Marcy frowned. "But…she's not really dangerous, is she? I mean, if she shows up…should I call security or something?"

"Don't do anything!" he yelled, knowing he had to get to Chloe, fast. "I'm leaving. I may not be back today. Don't say anything to anybody. Not a word. Or I will fire you so fast—"

Marcy clamped a hand over her mouth, nodding still.

Around the same time as Marcy was being read the riot act, Chloe had just gotten out of the shower. She could hear Robbie bursting into her room, calling her name. She tucked her towel more securely around herself and opened the bathroom door. "What's wrong now?"

"You tell me," he said. "Addie's having some sort of fit about James. What did he do?"

Chloe frowned. "He didn't do anything."

"You are such a bad liar. Why do you even try?" He took her by the arm and led her over to her bed, pushed her down and then sat facing her. "Now tell me everything, so I can tell you what to do."

"He…he just…he rubbed my feet."

Robbie gave her a truly odd look, like feet-rubbing might be some euphemism for an odd new sexual behavior. It wasn't. Was it?

"Chloe, no foot massage is that good," Robbie claimed.

"He just has these great hands, and the way he touches me.... You know how some people just know how to touch you? How fast, how slow, how soft, how hard, just...so it feels exactly right?"

Robbie looked wistful and a little depressed. "Not anything I've experienced recently, but yes."

"Well, James knows. Do you think he makes every woman he touches feel that way? Or is it just me? That there's something about him and what he does that fits with something in me and exactly how I want a man to touch me?"

"I have no idea," Robbie said, looking really freaked out now.

"Because, if it's just him and me? And it wouldn't feel that perfect with anyone else, I don't know how I can give that up, because it just feels so good."

It was a horrible thought. Just him. Nobody else?

"Ahh, dammit," Robbie said, but he gave her a big hug at the same time.

"How does a woman give that up?" she said. "To know there's someone in the world who can make you feel like that, and to just...walk away from it?"

"You do it because he makes you miserable everywhere but in bed," Robbie explained. "Because you can't trust him, and he's pushy and overbearing and selfish and couldn't stay with the same woman for a month if he tried."

Chloe shook her head, her tears falling now despite her best efforts not to cry. "He says he never cheated on me."

"Of course he said that. All men say that when they're trying to get you back."

"You're right."

"And then there's that whole question of what, exactly, equals cheating to certain people. What body parts can come into contact with what other body parts without cheating occurring? Hands? Mouths? Anything else? These are questions you want answered in detail by a man who claims he never cheated on you."

"Robbie, stop!"

"Too much information?"

"Definitely too much."

"Sorry."

"I have to remember how awful it was in the end," she said, feeling bleak. "How awful he made me feel."

"Yes. That. Keep that thought in your head, and you'll be fine. If that doesn't work, come and get me. I'll remind you. And Addie'll beat him up for you. What in the world did you tell her?"

Chloe sniffled, feeling especially pitiful about that. "That I know what he's up to. That he wants me back."

Robbie swore. "Well, he can't have you!"

Robbie finally left, but not ten minutes later, as Chloe was searching for something to wear, she heard a commotion, pounding feet sounded on the stairs, men's voices, and then James burst into her room.

"Chloe, you can't believe her, okay? At least not without hearing me out," he said.

Robbie came into the room and glared at James. "You want me to get rid of him?"

James scoffed at the idea that Robbie could make him leave.

"Oh, stop it, both of you! I thought we were being invaded by crazy brides again." She turned to Robbie. "Thank you, but I can do this, I promise. I'm feeling much better now."

"At least put some clothes on," Robbie whispered to her as he walked past her.

"I will," Chloe promised, clutching her towel to her with both hands.

He left, and James just stood there, looking oddly mussed up and just not as perfectly put together as he normally was. He was breathing hard, too.

"Don't believe her, okay? Just promise me you won't automatically believe her."

"Believe who?" she asked.

"Marcy. She doesn't know what she's talking about."

Marcy? He'd mentioned her before. "I haven't talked to your assistant."

"I know. I didn't think you did. Addie did. And I know what Marcy told her, and I'm telling you, please, don't believe it. Because she doesn't know what she's talking about this time."

Chloe frowned. "I don't know what your assistant told Addie."

"You don't?" He looked like he'd love to believe that, but couldn't quite bring himself to. "Really?"

"Really," she told him.

He let out a long, slow breath and then looked her over slowly from head to toe, like he'd just figured out she was standing there in nothing but a towel. And like he was really glad, either that she didn't know what this Marcy woman had told Addie or that Chloe wasn't wearing anything but a towel.

"I just...I couldn't stand the idea of you thinking that about me," he said.

"Thinking what?"

"That I didn't mean what I said to you last night. I really have missed you. I wish we could go back in time, and everything between us could have been different."

"James, you don't mean that."

"I do. I meant it all. Every word. You know, the happi-

est day of my life since we broke up was when your customers rioted at your store—"

"Oh, gee. Thanks."

"No. No. Not like that! I mean, that was the moment.
The moment when I gave up on staying away from you.
Ever since I saw your picture in the tabloids for that crazy
runway brawl thing, I've wanted to come see you again."

Chloe wanted so badly to believe that.

"Before that, even. I did. But I fought against it," he said.
"Because it hurt so much to lose you. And I kept fighting
with everything I had until the bride riot, and then I just
gave up."

She wanted to give up, too, and just be happy he was
back.

"When I knew I was going to see you again, I was
so damned happy. No more fighting it. No more holding
back."

Then he pulled her into his arms like he'd die right then
and there if he didn't. He backed her up against the wall
and pinned her with his body. She let him take her face in
his hands, nuzzle her cheek with the tip of his nose, nibble
on her ear a bit, and she could feel the smile on his lips,
lips that were waiting patiently a breath away from hers.

She whimpered and shifted against him, something
that only served to make her more aware of every inch of
the big, solid body pressed up against hers. She put up her
hands between them to hold him off, but mostly all they
ended up doing was soaking up the warmth of his body
and then slipping beneath his jacket to wrap around his
waist and hold him to her.

He teased mercilessly, the tip of his tongue messing
with her ear and making her shiver, his teeth taking a little,
bitty bite of her earlobe, tiny kisses making a path down
her cheek, to her chin, then back up to the tip of her nose

and finally landing on her mouth. His tongue teased ever so gently against the seam of her closed lips.

"Chloe, let me in," he whispered.

She shook her head just a bit.

He took her top lip and pulled it into his mouth, sucking on it, stroking it with his tongue, so sweet, so gentle. "Let me in."

Inside, her heart thrummed like a big bass drum, the beats echoing all through her body, her breathing shallow and fast. She had no defenses against the man, and it was so unfair, and yet it was wonderful. Like more feeling than anyone could stand, like drowning in it, being carried off by the current of it.

"It's not fair," she whispered finally.

"What's not fair?" he asked, his forehead resting against hers, his nose nuzzling against hers, his lips right there, waiting for her.

"How much I want you," she admitted.

"But that's a good thing."

"No, it's not. It makes me not able to think, not remember to be careful and protect myself from you."

"Chloe, I swear, the last thing in the world I want to do is hurt you. And the thing I want most in the whole, entire world right now is to have another chance with you. And I think you want that, too."

"Because of some weird ego thing? Because women don't say no to you, and I did?"

"No! Because when we were together, it was so good. It was a little bit crazy and scary, and I didn't handle it well. I freely admit that. But it was so good. If I hadn't been so stubborn or so proud, I'd have been back here a year and a half ago, begging you to take me back. I was just so stupid about the whole thing."

She shook her head. "You're not stupid about anything."

"I am about this. About women, I am—"

"You breeze through relationships with women—"

"Okay, women who don't mean anything to me," he admitted. "Women I can take or leave without really caring. Those, I can handle. I'm good at that."

She knew that. Sore subject.

"But with a woman who's truly important to me," he said, "one I really care about? One who scares me and makes me furious, and makes me feel like there is a life outside of work and that maybe I want one? With that woman, I'm a complete mess. And you know how much I hate to admit not knowing anything, not being able to handle anything, so you know what it costs me to tell you that."

She scoffed at that. "So you're telling me that I'm different from all the others? That's the oldest line in the book, James."

"It's not a line. It's the truth. Is it so impossible for you to believe I was crazy about you? And that I still am? I mean, look at me. I was a mess with you. Do you think that's how things normally are between me and a woman?"

"No—"

"Okay, there you go. That should tell you something."

Chloe blinked up at him. Either she really wanted to believe him, or he was starting to make sense. She honestly wasn't sure which.

"I don't know how to handle you—"

"I don't want to be handled," she said.

"Okay, what do you want? God, just tell me, and I'll do it. I'll do anything, Chloe. I swear, I want this that much. Just tell me what to do."

"Don't...don't scare me," she said finally.

He frowned. "How do I do that?"

"Don't push so hard."

"Okay," he said, backing off so that he wasn't touching her at all.

She grabbed at her towel, still between them but not as securely around her body as before. "And don't rush me."

He took a breath and let it out in a big whoosh. "You want to go out or something? Dinner? Drinks? A walk? What?"

"I don't know. I just…don't grab me and kiss me. Don't rub my feet. Don't look so damned perfect and get me alone in the back of a dark limousine with that privacy window up between us and the driver."

"Okay," he agreed, but he was grinning now, thinking he'd won.

"And don't…just don't…make me want you so much."

"Chloe, I swear, I want *you* so much I can hardly breathe. Just to hold you, to put my nose against your skin and breathe you in, to have my hands on your skin, any little bit of skin…."

"Okay, that's not the way to do it. To keep me from wanting you so much."

"Sorry. I'm completely out of my element here, I swear. It's not some kind of fake line. I don't know what to do. I'm worried I'll mess things up so badly in the next moment that I ruin everything, and I can't stand to do that. It's taken so long just to get back here and to think we'll have another chance together."

"Okay. Enough." She held up a hand to stop him from saying any more.

"I'm sorry. I just don't know how to do it. That whole normal relationship thing—"

"Well, I don't know how to do it, either," she said. "You know I don't! Nobody in my family knows how to do it. We didn't get that relationship gene. We got the relationship-disaster gene."

"So what do we do?"

"I don't know. Go slow, maybe?"

He looked like the thought was extremely painful. "Okay. I probably shouldn't touch you then."

Chloe nodded. That sounded reasonable. It made her a little sad, but she couldn't argue the wisdom of it.

"We could…take a walk," she suggested. "In public. No public displays of affection whatsoever."

"Okay. I'll do it."

"Have some coffee, talk…. I think that's the place to start."

"Okay. God, I've missed you."

He said his world had nearly come to an end without her, and there'd been a time when she'd felt the same way without him.

"That's really not the kind of talk I meant," she told him.

"You're right. I slipped, but I'll do better."

"Okay," she agreed.

He nodded. "So that's it? We're going to try this? You're going to give us another chance?"

"Yes."

She watched as the most beautiful smile came across his face. He had dimples in his cheeks, and they were irresistible. He looked like a thousand-pound weight had come off his shoulders, like the sun had come out after a thousand and one incredibly dreary days.

Did it really mean that much to him? To have her give them another chance? Even as cynical as she was, Chloe didn't think anyone could fake that look of complete joy.

And it scared her even more.

She swayed a little on her feet, her head spinning.

He really meant it?

"Hey? What is it? Are you all right?" he asked, beside her but not touching her.

"Yeah. I mean…"

And then she fell into his arms, all the strength going out of her limbs.

He caught her to him, lifted her easily and had her on the bed in seconds, feeling her forehead. "Do you have a fever?"

"No, I don't think so."

He stretched out on the bed beside her, lying on his side, and held up two fingers in front of her face. "How many?"

"Two. I just got dizzy for a second. That's all." He'd been so honest with her. She felt like she owed it to him to be honest in return. "You scare me, too."

"Oh, Chloe," he said, reaching for her, then pulling back.

"And it's not easy for me, either. It's so hard. Like being on top of a really tall building and someone wanting you to walk out onto the edge and stand there." She felt it again, the room tilting on its axis. "You make my head spin."

"Don't look down."

"I can't help it."

"I'll be so careful this time, I swear."

"Okay."

And then they both went still, smiling at each other, staring, thinking. Hearts pounding, breath ragged, something that felt like static electricity zipping between them.

If she touched him, she'd feel that little spark she'd felt the very first time, she knew it. The first time he'd kissed her, too, there'd been that distinctive electrical jolt when their lips met. She'd lain in her bed later that night, alone, her fingers on that point on her lips, still feeling that little buzz.

It had been like something out of a fairy tale, something

that definitely couldn't have been real, she'd reasoned with herself. Those kinds of things didn't happen in the real world.

"The first time you kissed me," she began, because she just had to know. "I know this sounds crazy, but…did it feel like—"

"A little buzz of electricity, except in the best possible way," he admitted. "I told myself I must have imagined it."

"Me, too."

"And it's still there. I can feel it right now."

She nodded. "It is. Maybe we're both just crazy, but…"

She lifted her hand up and he did the same until their hands were spread wide, lined up palm to palm, fingertips to fingertips, but not quite touching, and there it was, like a force field all their own, tingling between them.

"It's a trick," she tried to tell him. "Some trick kids do. I can't remember exactly how or why it works, but…it's just a trick."

He pushed his hand forward, and she pulled hers back, feeling a push not of him but of the energy between them. He looked very satisfied with himself when she stopped pulling away.

"Tell me to go, Chloe. Tell me right now."

"You have to. Really. You have to just go."

"And I shouldn't…maybe…get just one kiss? A good-bye kiss? Before I go?"

"You'll go then?" she asked. "Really?"

"I will. I swear."

The problem was, what exactly constituted one kiss?

He nibbled on her, so delicately, with his lips on hers, and then teased with his tongue. She didn't move, couldn't move, didn't want to. Not ever.

He spread out on top of her on the bed, his body a glorious weight, the scent of him, the heat, enveloping her, and still, he was barely kissing her. He'd dip his mouth down to hers and then retreat. She started lifting her head off the bed, chasing his mouth as he pulled away from her, and finally, she took his head in her hands and with a groan, pulled him to her.

He still moved with excruciating gentleness, still ever so slowly.

Heat bloomed inside her, a million senses coming to life, like he'd flipped a switch and she was immediately an achingly sexual being once again. She'd forgotten just how much he could make her want him.

He finally kissed her for real, fully, deeply, wickedly, and she thought she might die from the sheer pleasure of it, that there was no hope for her, no way she was letting him leave without both of them getting naked right here, right now.

"You are a wicked man," she said.

"Yes, I am, but I'm also leaving," he claimed, breathing hard. "You made me promise, and I'm not going to start out by breaking a promise to you."

"I take it all back! Don't go!"

"Chloe, I've waited too long for another chance with you. I'm not going to blow it now," he said, rolling over onto his side next to her.

"But...but—"

He tugged her towel up higher on her chest, tucked one end into the top edge, to hold it there. She hadn't quite lost the only thing she had on, but she'd come close.

"I'm a man of remarkable restraint. Remember that. I think I should get two kisses the next time we're together."

"Two?" He'd had about a thousand, tiny, sweet ones, and at least one gigantic, luxurious one. What would two of those be like? "Okay, two."

"Good. Tell me to go. Make me go, now, please."

She kissed him instead, thinking it was goodbye, after all, and a man should get a goodbye kiss. So she took his face in her hands and leaned onto her side and took his mouth with hers, needing one more time to feel that magic little zing of happiness and desire that was uniquely him.

He was being very, very good, not pushing, not rushing her at all, just letting her take what she wanted from him, and then she felt his hand on her thigh, sliding slowly up under the towel.

"Oops," he said.

She laughed. "Oops."

The hand stopped moving, but stayed where it was.

"It's really not fair that you've been naked this whole time. I mean...not fair! I'm just a man."

"Of remarkable restraint. You just told me so."

"Yeah, and then you had to go and take advantage of me."

"Yes, I did," she admitted. "I'm very bad."

"Chloe, I swear, if you don't shove me out the door soon, I'm going to have my hand on your bare bottom. You know how much I love that cute little bottom of yours, and then your towel is going to be gone completely, and I'm going to have my mouth all over you. Your choice. What's it going to be?"

She thought about that big, hot hand cupping one of her hips, rubbing along that curve. It would feel so good. He swore softly and was reaching for the towel, when she became aware, vaguely, of footsteps on the stairs, racing up the stairs. What in the...

The door to her room burst open, and Robbie stood there once again.

Chapter Seven

"I just got the most bizarre phone call from the police station—" Robbie stopped midsentence when he saw the two of them there, rolling around on Chloe's bed, Chloe in nothing but a precariously positioned towel. "What... are you doing?"

"I...we...arguing, mostly," Chloe said, securing her towel once again and sitting up on the bed.

"Yeah, right," Robbie said, glaring at James.

"Did you say the police?" asked James, who'd gotten to his feet and was straightening his tie.

Robbie blinked once, then again, like it was all just too much for him. "Yes, the police. Am I dreaming?"

"I don't think so," Chloe said, although now that she thought about all the things James had said, the absolutely perfect things, maybe they were all dreaming. She looked to James. "Are we dreaming?"

"I've dreamed about you," he admitted, looking very, very happy.

Okay, that was not helping. Chloe turned back to Robbie. "Tell us what you think the police said."

"That they had Addie there," Robbie said. "And that she'd been arrested at James's office building. He owns the whole building?"

"I'm in a partnership that owns the building. I'm the managing partner," he said. "Why would Addie be at my office? Why would anyone there arrest her?"

"Something about a disturbance, a security guard and another woman," Robbie said.

"Addie has a thing for a security guard at my office?" James asked.

"No," Chloe said. "She doesn't have a thing for anyone at the moment. If she did, I'd know."

"So why would she be at my office?" James asked.

"She was really mad at you about last night," Chloe said.

"Wait," Robbie jumped in. "What happened last night?"

"Nothing," Chloe and James said at the same time.

"Oh, right!" Robbie didn't believe that.

"Hey, I didn't do anything last night," James protested.

"You…you…you rubbed my feet," Chloe said.

He threw his hands up in the air. "Like that's some sort of crime?"

"It is when you do it to…you know why you did it! You wanted me all relaxed and happy, so you could…you know!" Chloe insisted.

"No, I don't know. You wear those silly shoes all night, and your feet are bound to hurt. I know that—"

"From all those other women you date. You rub all their feet? You think I want to hear about other women you've been with, rubbing your feet and teaching you how to rub theirs? I don't want to hear that. No woman does—"

"Wait a minute," Robbie cut in. "Rubbing your feet? Is

that some euphemism for some kinky thing I don't know about?"

"No. At least, not that I know of," Chloe told him, then turned back to James.

"I'm not into anything weird. You know that," he protested.

"You know exactly what you were trying to do last night. You wanted me all relaxed and unsuspecting, so you could try to make me admit...what I admitted today!"

"No, I did not! I just thought your feet must hurt, and that they were one part of your body you might actually let me touch. And...yeah, maybe I thought I'd start there and end up...touching other places, and if that happened, I wouldn't have objected. But it would have just happened. That's all. That's what men are like. That's what we do. Start touching here, maybe work your way there."

"Okay, he's right about that," Robbie agreed.

"Yeah," James said. "Besides, I wasn't thinking about trying to get you to admit anything until you made me mad, and then...well, I was just mad."

"Well, I was mad, too, and Addie knew it. I guess...she might have...come up with some of her own ideas about why I was mad and about some things she might want to say to you about it."

"Okay, but that still doesn't explain her ending up in jail," James said.

Chloe frowned, then looked to Robbie. "They really said she was in jail?"

"Unless I imagined the whole thing. Weird thing to imagine, though."

"Yeah," Chloe said.

James's phone rang. He looked at it and said, "Hang on. Caller ID says it's the police."

As he listened, he began to look as confused as Robbie

when he'd first burst into the room. When he got off the phone, he said, "Okay, they say they've arrested Marcy, too."

"Addie and your assistant?"

"Well, we've never had anyone arrested in the lobby before. So, I'd say the odds of it happening twice in one day—in unrelated incidents—are highly unlikely."

"Addie's really going to hate you now," Robbie said.

It took an hour and a half to find them and pay their bail. The wait for them to actually be processed out was even longer.

The police didn't say much, just something about a woman wanting access to James's office, James's assistant refusing to allow that, and a security guard stepping between them, and then some sort of minor scuffle.

"Cat fight," one of the officers had told James and Robbie, grinning.

When they were alone, waiting, James said, "Marcy's father is a friend of mine and a business associate. When she got out of school, he begged me to give her a job, and I did. She's a little weird. She can be a little high-strung at times, but she's never been violent."

"Neither has Addie."

James's assistant got out of jail first. At least, Chloe assumed it was his assistant. She hoped he didn't know anyone else in jail today.

She was wearing an expensive if very boring suit, her long brown hair in a knot, but with more of it falling down now than actually in the knot. She had big, black streaks of mascara running down her face, was wearing only one shoe and looked terrified as she walked slowly toward them.

James looked incredulous. "Marcy?"

"I am so sorry," Marcy whispered furiously. "So, so, so sorry. And I know you're probably going to fire me. I understand that. I just…I just…I…"

And then she started sobbing pitifully.

James, looking exasperated, put his arm around her, patted her shoulder and let her cry it out. When her sobs finally slowed, he said, "What the hell happened?"

"It was Wayne, the new security guard. You know, the big, not-so-smart one who kind of has a crush on me?"

"No, Marcy, I don't know which one has a crush on you."

"Well, he can be kind of—" She stopped, mouth hanging open. "Oh, my God, it's you! You're Chloe! I've been wanting so much to meet you—"

"Marcy, not now!" James said.

"Oh, right. I'm sorry. I just, I've never met anybody who was on the cover of all those tabloids before. Or on *Entertainment Tonight*."

James winced and mouthed, "Sorry."

Chloe nodded and managed a smile for poor Marcy, who seemed a little flaky, but mostly just terribly young.

"You're so much prettier than you were in those pictures or the videos of that awful brawl—"

"Marcy, shut up about all that!" James told her.

"Oh, right. Sorry. I just…" She kept staring at Chloe, then got all worried again. "Oh, my God, was that really your sister I got arrested with? Please, please, please tell me it wasn't."

"If it wasn't, the police say she had my sister's driver's license and looked enough like her to pass for Addie," Chloe told her.

Marcy looked devastated. "I just don't know how this could have happened."

"Neither do I," James said. "Start talking, and stick to the subject this time. What happened?"

"I spoke with someone this morning claiming to be Ms. Allen's assistant, needing urgently to speak to you, saying among other things that she…wanted to do bodily harm to you—"

"Sounds like Addie," James said.

Marcy looked even more hopeless than before. "And I was a little uneasy about the conversation. So I called downstairs to security and got Wayne…." Marcy sighed heavily and looked at Chloe. "Why can't men be both intelligent and great-looking? I mean, I couldn't go out with anybody like Wayne. What would we have to talk about? But sometimes, I think I could just sit there and look at him for hours and—"

"Marcy, nobody cares what's going on with you and Wayne!"

"Right. Sorry," she said. "I told him to watch out for a suspicious woman who would try anything to get to see my boss, and Wayne said that someone had been lurking around downstairs all morning, not trying to get upstairs to any of the offices, just watching everyone go in and out. And I thought that sounded like someone from one of the tabloids, you know, spying on us all."

"Of course," James said.

"Then, a few minutes later, Wayne called back, and I…I—"

"Despite me ordering you not to do or say anything to anyone—"

"I know." Marcy winced. "But I thought if you were going to fire me anyway, I might as well at least try to fix things. So I went downstairs."

"And made them so much worse," James said. "I can't

believe you graduated from Wharton. Did you really, Marcy?"

"I did. I swear!" Marcy's lower lip started trembling. She was going to cry again, right here in the police station. She mouthed to Chloe, behind James's back, "Please, ask him not to fire me. I love my job."

Chloe nodded that she would, feeling sorry for the young woman and knowing what it was like to watch your career hopes dashed.

"Thank you," Marcy mouthed.

And then Addie burst into the lobby, looking as disheveled as Marcy and more mad than scared. She zeroed in on Chloe, then spotted James, and it was like smoke was coming out of her ears, she was so enraged.

Marcy slid behind James, whimpering, "Please don't let her hurt me."

Addie marched over, got up in James's face, pointing at Marcy. "This idiot child and that hulk of a security guard work for you?"

"Yes," James admitted. "Could we please not do this in public? That's all I'm asking, Addie. Please."

"Because some tabloid reporter might be lurking around?" Addie scoffed at that. "That's what she kept saying! That's what started this mess."

"You scared me, and Wayne thought you were going to hurt me! That's really all it was, I swear, Mr. Elliott. She came charging toward me, and Wayne was just trying to protect me," Marcy said, peering around James's shoulder just long enough to put her two cents in.

"That big buffoon of a rent-a-cop grabbed me and literally picked me up off my feet!"

"He just didn't want you to hurt anybody!" Marcy whined.

"I don't hurt people! I'm not some kind of nut! I'm

Chloe's sister! All I wanted was for the hulk to put me down!"

James stood between the two of them as they leaned left and right to yell around him. "This is a nightmare!" He turned to Marcy. "Say one more word, and you're fired. I mean it."

Marcy slunk down behind him and stayed there.

To Addie, he said, "Please, I am begging you. I have a car and driver outside. Could we please just get in the car and finish this there?"

"Not with her," Addie said, trying to look around him to get to Marcy.

"Fine. Marcy, go home. Right now. I'll hail you a taxi and talk to you tomorrow." He looked to Chloe and Addie. "Ladies, this way, please."

They marched out of the police station together, Addie still fuming, Marcy pouting, James exasperated, Chloe thinking her life could not get any weirder. Tabloid reporters, YouTube videos, the Bride Blog, Bryce, Eloise, her beautiful dresses that people believed were cursed.

They made it to the car with only a few more pointed comments from Addie, Marcy pouting and slinking away into a cab idling by the curb. Chloe just wanted to hide, and definitely not be caught between Addie, James and the fight she knew they were going to have.

"James," she said, "Addie and I are going to get a taxi and go home."

"No, he and I are going to talk. I was attacked in the foyer of his office by some rent-a-goon and his crazy assistant!" Addie yelled.

Chloe held up her hand. "Okay. You can tell me all about it. I just…I can't listen to the two of you go at each other right now. Please?"

James, looking like he absolutely hated the idea, leaned

in close and whispered, "She's going to give you a million reasons why you should run as fast as you can away from me right now and never see me again."

"I know, but she won't convince me to stay away from you. I promise."

"I'm going to hold you to that," he said, leaning in to talk to his driver for a moment, then holding open the car door for Chloe. "Here, you two take my car. The driver has the address."

"Thank you," Chloe said, not looking forward to the ride alone with Addie, either, but grateful to avoid all-out war between Addie and James.

But Addie wasn't done. She stood there, glaring at James.

"Addie, get in," Chloe said.

"No!"

"If you don't get in, I'll ask James to, and we'll leave you to find your own way home."

Addie gaped at her. "I just got arrested because of him!"

"Get in or I'm leaving you," Chloe insisted.

Addie got in. She was furious, but inside the car.

James shot Chloe one last worried look, closed the door and watched them drive away.

"He is like poison to you," Addie said, delivering her opening salvo the minute they pulled into traffic.

"I know. Don't you think I know that? I just can't help it. I'm crazy about him."

"Yes, exactly. Crazy. No one should be crazy over a man. It's a bad thing. You should know this by now."

"I do. I just…I've missed him so much. You were right. I latched on to Bryce so fast because I wasn't over James. I felt so bad, and I needed so much to forget about him, and then there was Bryce, trying to go completely straight for some reason. I bet it was that aunt of his with all the money and no kids of her own. He was always trying to impress her, and she's ultraconservative." Chloe felt even worse now. "Maybe he was going to marry me to make his aunt think he was straight, so she'd leave him all her money."

"Who knows why he did it? He's a man. They'll lie about anything."

Chloe shot her a look that said she was not helping right now. "Anyway, I jumped right into a relationship with him, and now I'm paying for it. But it brought James back into my life, and…God, Addie, I just can't be sorry about that."

Addie gaped at her. "It's that bad? Already?"

Chloe nodded, admitting it.

"I went there to tell him that he couldn't do this to you again, that I'd hurt him if he so much as tried, and it's already too late?"

"It is. I'm sorry. I tried so hard to get over him, and I tried to resist him. But what if…there's no way to really resist him? I mean…what if he's the one? The only one?"

Addie shook her head, silent for a moment, speechless.

Yeah, it was that bad, that big and overwhelming and scary.

"We need to get you on a plane," Addie said finally. "To anywhere. Anywhere but here."

"I can't leave now. We have to try to save the business. And besides, even if I did leave, he'd just come find me. He really wants another chance with me—"

"And you believe him? You think he actually means that?"

Chloe nodded.

"You know that's crazy. You know how he is with women. Admit it—you've been secretly keeping track of all the gossip about him and whatever ridiculous, beautiful woman he's dating at the moment."

"Yes, I have."

"And last time, in the end, you caught him red-handed with that model, Giselle—"

"I know."

"Men don't change," Addie said softly, taking Chloe's hand in hers as she said it, the awful truth.

"But it's not...impossible for a man to change," Chloe tried.

"Oh, God! He's got you again. He's got you right where he wants you."

And to that, Chloe couldn't say anything.

It was true.

James awoke refreshed, renewed and determined to see Chloe and make sure Addie hadn't convinced her that he was the devil incarnate, come to ruin her life in every way possible.

He put on his favorite suit, then added a shirt in the palest of blues, because Chloe used to always try to get him to mix it up a little with some colors. Going with a very pale blue instead of white was big for him. He was trying to show her he could be flexible and a little daring. He even put on a striped tie instead of a solid-colored one— another huge wardrobe concession.

He walked up to the newsstand that morning happy, confident, excited for the day to come and what it would bring.

Vince gave him an odd look, he noticed, but he wasn't worried. It was probably because of the striped tie. Then James saw that Vince had another tabloid waiting for him.

For just a moment, James felt a little jab of anxiety.

But no. Everything was fine. He was sure of it.

He stood directly in front of Vince. No mistaking that odd look now. And Vince laid the tabloid down on the

counter in front of James. The headline read Chloe in a
Three-Way (Fight) for One of New York's Most Eligible!
Her Sister and His Assistant Caught Naked With Him,
Financial District Brawl Results.

James went absolutely still, barely even breathing.

Just the day before, things had been going so well. He'd
been in Chloe's bed, kissing her, hearing her promise to
give him another chance, and then Robbie had burst in
talking about Addie being in jail.

Now, somehow, there was a picture of him, Chloe,
Addie and Marcy outside the police station, Addie looking
like she was going to kill him, Marcy pouting and Chloe…
poor Chloe, looking so sad. Below that was a smaller one
of Addie and Marcy in handcuffs, being hauled out of the
foyer of James's office.

Chapter Eight

"No, no, no!" James shook his head. "It can't be. Tell me you made it up, Vince. Tell me you have a friend who can put things like this together, and that the whole thing is a really bad joke! Please, tell me that."

Vince looked like he even felt sorry for James. "Tough break, man. The three of them finding out about each other like that. What are you gonna do?"

"I didn't do it!" James held up the stupid tabloid. "I'm not sleeping with my assistant or Chloe's sister. Hell, I'm not even sleeping with Chloe yet."

"No way I believe that," Vince said. "I saw the picture of you and that Chloe girl where it looked like you were undressing her with your teeth!"

"Well, I didn't. Okay, a little undressing with the teeth, but that was it. She doesn't trust me yet. God, she may never trust me again."

James just stood there, stunned and furious. This was a

disaster. There was the whole public humiliation aspect of it for Chloe. Having tabloids blaring to the world the news that the man who was supposed to love you was sneaking around behind your back would no doubt mean a reprisal of the whole cursed-in-love thing for Chloe and her business.

"I'm telling you, sex with a relative or a best friend of your lady? Strictly off-limits," Vince said.

James didn't even try to explain. And perhaps for one time in his life, he had no idea what to do next. It was the most horrible feeling. He always knew what to do. He always had a plan. The highly developed sense of logic he'd always counted on, the ability to step back from any situation, weigh the information, the variables, the probabilities and know the right thing to do... It was gone. Just... gone.

It was Chloe, Chloe World, Chloe Chaos. Logic did not apply. Plans went horribly awry. Confusion reigned. And yet he desperately wanted to be with her. He felt utterly defeated in that moment, James Elliott IV, a man who believed he could do anything, solve any problem, make anything work.

"I was supposed to fix things for her. I was just trying to help."

"By sleeping with her and her sister?" Vince gave a dismissive huff.

"I am not sleeping with her sister!" James yelled.

People on the street were starting to pause and stare. And that's when James saw the flash.

Right in his face.

A camera flash!

Some tabloid photographer was tailing him now!

"Oh, you bastard!" James yelled, taking off after the

guy, who continued snapping shots in James's face and backing up furiously as James charged toward him.

He was going to grab that camera and shove it down the guy's throat if it was the last thing he did. That was all he was thinking about. Get the guy, get the camera.

James took off, fury and maybe the flash of the camera blinding him at first. He stepped off the curb. The next thing he knew, a bike messenger was practically on top of him, people were screaming and he felt oddly like he was flying through the air.

Marcy felt certain Mr. Elliott intended to fire her after the incident with Addie, but she went to work anyway. He said they'd talk today, presumably so he could bawl her out in detail and then fire her. She wanted that to be a face-to-face meeting. Not that she'd rather be fired in person. She'd just rather be able to plead her case to keep her job in person. Marcy wasn't above begging.

On the way, she made her usual newsstand stop for copies of all the relevant tabloids, and that's when she saw it, right there on the cover of the *New York Mirror*.

"Oh, my God, that's me!" she yelled.

People started staring, whispering.

The newsstand guy took the tabloid from her hands and held it up next to her face. "Yeah, I guess it does look a little like you."

"No, it really is me!" There was a zing of absolute glee at first. Her picture was right there, like she was some kind of celebrity!

But then it occurred to her that the only potentially tabloid-worthy thing she'd done was end up in jail the day before with Ms. Allen's sister.

Marcy gaped at the photo, a horrible feeling of dread moving through her body. It showed her, Addie and Chloe outside the police station, with a headline that implied they were all sleeping with Marcy's boss, and that poor Ms. Allen was, indeed, cursed in love once again.

"Sleepin' with your boss. Never a good idea," the news-stand guy said.

"I am not sleeping with my boss!" Marcy yelled back, which only made more people turn and stare.

She rushed down the street and into her office build-ing, where she came face-to-face with Wayne, who looked quite miffed at her.

"You're sleeping with Mr. Elliott?" he yelled.

"No! I'm not," she claimed.

"I can read, Marcy," he said, holding up the offending tabloid.

Marcy whimpered. Her cell phone rang. When she grabbed it to avoid seeing the condemnation in Wayne's eyes, the caller ID indicated it was her mother.

"Oh, no!" she cried. "My mother's seen that!"

Her mother didn't read silly gossip, but she had friends who did.

Somehow she got herself upstairs and walked into the office, only to find everyone there staring, too, and shoot-ing her many disapproving looks.

"I didn't do it!" she cried. "I swear!"

They kept staring. She grabbed a ringing phone. To have something to do. And that's how she found out that her boss was in the emergency room.

Chloe and Addie were in the kitchen waiting for the first pot of coffee to finish brewing, when Addie's phone rang.

"I can't believe she has the nerve to call me again!" Addie said.

"Who?" Chloe asked.

"That crazy Marcy woman who works for James." Addie clicked a button to answer the call and said, "What in the world could you—"

Chloe watched as Addie frowned, then looked seriously freaked out and then just yelled, "What?" And with that, the familiar ooze of dread started working its way through Chloe's body.

Addie clicked off the phone and said, "Okay, try not to freak out."

Chloe's mouth fell open. "Freak out? There's nothing left to freak out about! Please, tell me there's nothing left!"

"Marcy didn't have a lot of details, at least none that made sense. But James is in the E.R., and he's asking for you."

"James is hurt?" That was worse than anything she had imagined.

"Come on," Addie said, taking her by the arm. "I'll go with you."

After what seemed an eternity, they got to the E.R.

"You have a patient here, James Elliott, who's asking for me," Chloe told the desk clerk, who immediately put up a hand to tell her she'd have to wait to even ask a question.

Addie leaned around Chloe to stare into the corner. "Wait, there's Marcy."

They hadn't gotten anything out of Marcy that made sense before a nurse found them, asking Chloe to follow her. Chloe left Marcy and Addie whispering furiously to each other, definitely hiding something.

Gulping, she finally asked the nurse, "What happened to James?"

"Apparently, he stepped off the curb and got hit by—"

"Oh, my God!" Chloe cried.

"—a bike messenger," the nurse finished.

Chloe started to breathe again. Not a car. A bicycle.

Still, those guys rode like lunatics, zipping in and out of traffic the way they do.

"Yeah, I'd take one of those over getting hit by a car. Still, it's no picnic." The nurse headed down the hall, motioning for Chloe to follow.

She stopped at a cubicle, drew a curtain aside and there was James, lying on a stretcher, looking bruised and battered, scrapes here and there, a white bandage on his head, an IV line in one arm and cardiac leads on his bare chest, which also had a big red bruise on it.

Chloe gasped. "Are you sure it was just a bike?"

"Yes. There were several witnesses," the doctor, who was standing by the bed, told her, steering her to the side of the bed and a waiting stool. "Sit. I'm Dr. Morgan."

"Chloe Allen. What's wrong with him?"

"Hopefully just a concussion and some bruises, but we're still waiting for the scans to be read to be sure there's no internal bleeding. There are no obvious fractures, although I don't know how. His BP's okay. Might have a cardiac contusion—"

"Wait, his heart?"

"It may be bruised, yes."

That sounded like such a scary thing, a bruised heart, and so sad. Chloe felt like her heart was bruised, too, right then, just from looking at James.

"The main point of impact was the chest," the doctor said. "But right now, the EKG is fine. He was unconscious at the scene, which we never like when someone's taken a blow to the head. But he woke up in the ambulance and has been in and out here. And he really wants to talk to you."

"But he's going to be okay?"

"I want to see his scans come back clean, but right now,

I'm not too worried," the doctor said, then hesitated, giving Chloe an odd look.

"What? What is it?"

"We had a hard time calming him down when he got here," the doctor said. "So please don't say anything to upset him."

"Of course. I would never want to do anything to make him worse."

"Good," the doctor said, then turned to James. "And I think he's figured out that you're here. Mr. Elliott? We found Chloe for you. She's right here."

James turned his head slowly toward Chloe. Beneath the stark white bandage on his left temple, his gaze wasn't quite focusing and one eyelid was swollen. He reached for her, and she took his hand in hers, putting her other hand on his shoulder—the one that didn't have road rash on it.

"Chloe?" he said weakly. "I didn't do it, I swear."

"Okay." Chloe looked to the doctor, who nodded that yes, this was what she needed to do. "James, I'm sure whatever it is, it's fine."

"I really didn't. You have to believe me."

Chloe squeezed his hand, trying to reassure him. "I do. I promise."

"I didn't sleep with either one of those women, I swear."

The doctor froze at that. So did the nurse, both looking at Chloe worriedly.

James, now that he'd gotten all that out, gave her a little smile. Then he drifted off, helped along by whatever medication he was on.

Women?

What women?

She looked at the doctor, who seemed like he was still waiting and worrying about what Chloe might do or say.

The nurse seemed as if she'd just had a little lightbulb moment, looking at Chloe. "Oh, my God! You're her! That runway brawl woman! The one who's supposedly cursed in love? Wow, you really are, aren't you?"

Chloe couldn't say a thing. Not one single word.

Yes, she was *that* woman, wasn't she?

The doctor took the nurse by the arm and practically shoved her out of the cubicle. "I'm so sorry for that. It's the last thing you need right now. And thank you for being so calm and not upsetting the patient."

Chloe nodded, having absolutely nothing to say at the moment.

Who could he possibly have slept with?

And not one woman, but two? How did he find the time?

He'd seemed so sincere this time, and just crazy about her. Why bother, if he didn't really care for her at all? What was the point? Chloe sighed, looking down at that beautiful face of his, that hand she still held in hers.

She was cursed, no doubt about it.

Chloe was trying to stay calm as she headed back out to the waiting room, to not remember every other time in her life when she'd found out a man she thought she loved was sleeping with someone else. Then she heard what sounded very much like Addie's raised voice saying, "No, no, no. We don't need security! We'll behave."

She followed the sound of raised voices and found Addie, Marcy, two security guards and James's doctor, who looked horrified when he spied Chloe.

"What's wrong now?" Chloe asked.

"Nothing. It's all a misunderstanding," Addie tried to reassure her.

"That's what you said yesterday, when we ended up bailing you both out of jail." Too late she realized that might not be the best thing to say in front of the security guards, then added, "They're annoying and ridiculous at times, but not dangerous."

"You are not helping," Addie complained.

"Well, neither are you! Can't the two of you get along for five minutes while I'm trying to make sure James is okay?"

"Yeah. About James—" Addie began.

"Not now," Marcy cut in.

"Yes, now. It'll be even worse if she hears he's supposedly sleeping with two other women and doesn't hear that we're the two women in question."

Marcy thrust a copy of today's tabloid into Chloe's hands.

"Oh, that's perfect. Just perfect," Chloe said, humiliated anew as the doctor, the security guards and seemingly everyone in the waiting room was staring at her, some with curiosity and some in abject pity.

"I swear, I've never slept with him," Marcy said, then shot Addie a look.

"She knows I didn't sleep with him. I can't stand him," Addie said.

"Wait, the two women he supposedly slept with are you and Marcy?"

Marcy nodded, looking a bit scared. "He told you?"

Chloe laughed a bit, some of her tension dissipating. "It's really supposed to be the two of you?"

"I would just never do that! It's been awful already, having people think I did," Marcy said, then looked like she was about to cry. "My own mother thinks I did it!"

"Okay, enough," Chloe said. "The two of you get out of here, before you get into another fight and we all end up in jail or in another tabloid."

They left, finally, Marcy offering to return with clothes

for James to wear home. The doctor gave Chloe an odd look as he said, "You lead a very interesting life."

James was having absolutely bizarre dreams.

There were people fighting to hold him down, poking at him, shining big lights in his eyes, taking off his clothes, and then he woke to find himself on a stretcher in what looked like a hospital. *Weird. Very weird.*

He felt the IV needle in the back of his hand, the little pads on his chest hooked up by cables to a heart monitor. He didn't have a shirt on. He might not be wearing anything except a thin sheet. It hurt to breathe and to move his head. Just having a head, in fact, hurt.

Then he saw Chloe dozing, curled up in a chair by his side and holding his hand, which made everything better.

The last thing he remembered was walking down the street, on his way to work. Things came rushing at him in disjoined flashes. Vince at the newsstand. The tabloid. Him, Marcy, Addie and Chloe. Good God!

There was a beeping noise nearby, getting faster and faster.

His heart?

A nurse came in, checking the monitors. A doctor came in and did the same. Chloe woke, sat up and looked worried.

"Just relax," the doctor said, putting a stethoscope to James's chest and listening. "Lots of people come to in the hospital a little disoriented. The heart rate kicks up. No big deal."

"I'm on a heart monitor?"

"Just a precaution. Hurt to breathe?"

"Yes."

"That's probably why. Head hurt, too?"

"Yes."

"We think you hit your head when you landed. Remember anything?"

"I was…" At the newsstand. *God.* Did Chloe know what was in the tabloids this morning? He looked at her. She was holding his hand, looking concerned but trying to smile at him. "Uhh…I was walking to work. I stepped off the curb, and then…I was in the ambulance."

"Okay. Not bad. Sounds like you only lost a few minutes. Not unusual with concussions. You were hit by a guy on a bike. Could have been a lot worse and from what the witnesses said, not your fault. He was going the wrong way on a one-way street. Right now, you look good. We're going to watch you for a little while, wait for your scans to come back and then we'll know for sure."

James frowned. "What happened to the other guy?"

"Already walked out of here. He was wearing a helmet. And he landed on the trunk of a parked car, which is much more forgiving than asphalt."

"Okay. Thank you," he said to the doctor.

The doctor sent a cautious smile in Chloe's direction, then took the nurse—who looked like she might be taking notes for the tabloids tomorrow—by the arm and hauled her out of the cubicle. Then it was just James and Chloe, with all the privacy a curtain could provide.

He took a cautious look at her.

"You were on your way to work?"

"Yes." He nodded.

"Maybe buying your *Wall Street Journal?*"

"Yes." She knew? Wait a minute. Had he told her himself?

"James, please don't tell me you nearly got yourself killed over the tabloid shot of the four of us outside the jail yesterday."

Yeah, he had told her. Right here in the hospital.

"Chloe, you know it's not true, right?" He rushed on. "Me sleep with Addie? That would be like sleeping with a porcupine. Plus, she'd never agree to it, unless… To keep us apart? Oh, damn. She might actually do that if she thought it would keep you and me apart!"

"If she was truly desperate to keep you away from me and couldn't think of any other way… No, even then, I don't think she'd sleep with you."

"Addie hates me, and for once it's a good thing," he said, relieved. "Now, Marcy is really smart when it comes to finance, but at the same time, wacky and annoying. I'd rather jump off a building than sleep with her."

"She was horrified by the idea, herself. Poor thing. Apparently, her mother's seen the story. I think we may have cured Marcy's tabloid addiction."

"So, you and me? We're okay?"

"James, you can't have seriously believed I'd think you were sleeping with either Addie or Marcy—"

"I knew it would hurt you. That it would be humiliating for you and bring up bad memories of how we broke up the first time." He looked absolutely grim. "And I knew you probably wouldn't believe I'd have anything to do with Addie or Marcy, but what about anyone else?"

Chloe just looked away.

"Yeah, that's what I was thinking. That's what I was so afraid of. I know exactly how fragile this whole thing between us is right now," he said. "We've never been good at trusting each other. Hell, I'm not good at trusting anyone, and you just can't seem to trust men, and I know I'm part of the reason."

Chloe shook her head. "You're right. It's never going to be easy for either one of us."

He nodded. "If it had been anyone but Addie and Marcy I was supposed to be sleeping with, you'd have believed it and walked away from me again. That's what I thought when I saw that tabloid."

"I'm sorry. I'm so sorry you were hurt—"

"I'm fine, Chloe. And all I need to know is that we're going to get the time together we need to learn to trust each other again. I couldn't stand it if anything happened and we didn't get that time."

"We'll have time," she promised.

"I can control what I do, what I say, where I go, but those tabloids? They can say anything. We've already seen that. I'm scared of what they might say, and the last time we were together… Chloe, you would have believed I was sleeping with half the population of Manhattan."

She shook her head. "We're different people now. This is a different time—"

"No, it's not," he insisted. "I'm afraid, in many ways, we're the exact same people, making the exact same mistakes, and I don't want to do that again. Do you really want to do that all over again?"

"No," she admitted finally. "It was too hard. It hurt too much."

"Yes, it did."

Her gaze darted to his, old hurt still in her eyes and a little bit of a challenge, a little bit of disbelief. Did she really think it hadn't nearly killed him to lose her? Had he really made it look like he hadn't cared that much about her the first time they were together?

"We have to talk about this, Chloe. We have to talk about Giselle—"

"Not now. I can't do it now. It's been an awful day. I was so scared when I got the call that you'd been hurt."

He should make her listen. He knew it. But he was just so damned tired. Every bone in his body hurt. Hell, it still hurt to breathe.

"Come here, Chloe," he said, pulling her against him.

She came slowly, easing down to snuggle into his side, her palm flat against his chest, working its way between the leads of the EKG, then pressed a tiny kiss to his shoulder. "You really scared me."

"I know. I'm so sorry," he said. At times, she could be so fierce, such a little fireball, and at others, she could feel so tiny and vulnerable. He loved both those sides of her.

"This whole thing is getting out of hand," she argued. "You're just trying to help me and you almost died out there today."

"I didn't almost die—"

"Do you know how many pedestrians are killed in Manhattan every year—?"

"Okay, yes. But I'm fine. I swear." He felt her take a breath, deep and slow, and gave up on making her listen to him right then. "One day, when you're ready, you're going to listen to what I have to say about the night we broke up, and you're going to believe me, Chloe. And you're going to trust me again. And then, everything is going to be better."

"Okay. One day—"

"Before you leave. Promise me," he insisted.

"Okay, I promise. But right now, you're supposed to rest, not get upset. The doctor said so."

"All right." He let it go for then and finally started to relax, both reassured and comforted by the feel of her head against his shoulder. "Stay with me?"

"Of course I'll stay."

He could make it if she stayed.

Today had been so bizarre, so unbelievably bad, that feeling of flying through the air out on the street. The sound of people screaming now. Thinking he had to land at some point, land hard. People working over him on the street, in the ambulance.

He remembered being scared, and that all he'd wanted was Chloe. She was here now, cuddled up against him. So he closed his eyes, locked his arms around her and let himself rest.

Chapter Nine

After spending the entire day and part of the evening under observation in the E.R., James was finally discharged. He and Chloe sat side by side, holding hands and uncharacteristically silent in the car on the way to his apartment.

Chloe soon saw that it was the same one he'd lived in when they were together, as stark, modern, functional and completely impersonal as before. Colorless, too. How did anyone live without color?

He hesitated just inside the doorway, wincing as he flipped a switch and the light hit him. Chloe turned it back off. With the big expanse of windows in the living room, there was enough light from the street and surrounding buildings for them to see.

She was exhausted from the day, so she didn't really understand how he was still standing. Guiding him straight to his bedroom, she pulled back the covers of his starkly modern platform bed and gave him a pointed look.

"Don't even think about arguing with me on this."

"Chloe, I've wanted you back in my bed for a year and a half. Believe me, I'm not arguing."

She shot him an incredulous look. "You can barely move. I don't know what you think you're going to do in that bed tonight—"

"Hold you, if I'm very, very lucky," he said, then made the mistake of trying, too quickly, to slide his jacket off, and ended up grimacing.

She pushed his hands away and took it off him herself, hanging it up in his meticulously organized closet. She knew exactly where it went. When she came back to him, he'd loosened his tie. She took that, too, and hung it up. She was simply overcome by the need to take care of him. It was something he'd never let her—or anyone else, that she knew of—do for him.

She began undoing the buttons of his shirt, as she'd done that first night they'd met, when she still thought he was her model groom. And she could swear that touching him now, her fingertips barely brushing against his poor, bruised chest, was every bit as unsettling as it had been that first time.

"Going to tuck me in, too?" he asked softly.

"If you're lucky."

He grinned at her through the dim light in the bedroom. "I'm feeling very lucky right now."

Which unfortunately brought back the memory of the doctor telling him how very lucky he was. *Get pitched into the street instead of the sidewalk, and a car would likely have gotten you before you hit the ground. And you could have landed the wrong way.... It's a miracle you didn't break anything.*

Chloe felt a shiver work its way down her spine.

James's hands closed over hers, holding them against his chest for a moment, as he breathed in and out. Then he brought her hands to his lips, kissing them softly. "Don't think about it, Chloe. I'm fine."

She found she couldn't look him in the eye, concentrating again on unfastening the remaining buttons on his shirt, then undoing his cuffs. She eased the shirt off his shoulders, and before she could go put it away, he took it from her hands and dropped it on the floor.

His arms came gently around her, drawing her slowly and cautiously against him.

"I should go," she said. "You need to rest."

"So do you." He kissed her forehead, stroked a hand through her hair. "I don't think you should be alone tonight—"

"You don't think I should be alone tonight?"

"I think neither one of us needs to be, and I for damned sure don't want to be. Stay with me, Chloe. Just sleep beside me in the bed. Let me hold you all night, and in the morning, we'll talk. You promised we would. You promised to hear me out about Giselle."

She closed her eyes against the notion of the talk, that there was anything he could say that would truly make a difference. Was he going to lie to her again? Even now? Because, honestly, she'd seen him with that witch of a model, Giselle, seen them in each other's arms. It hadn't been some innocent embrace, and it had been the end of him and her.

How could she possibly want to be here with him this much when he'd hurt her the way he had back then? How could she think anything had truly changed? It was like getting run over by an eighteen-wheeler and just lying there on the street, asking the driver to back over you one more time for good measure.

She really wasn't that stupid, was she?

Okay, yes, she was that stupid, because she wanted to be in that bed with him.

James stood there with her in his arms, not letting go. If need and determination could keep her here, she wasn't leaving. But he knew, too, that he could only push so far before she either pushed back or ran away from him. He was damned sick and tired of her running away.

So he stood there, waiting, an odd kind of nervous energy buzzing through his body, years of reserve and caution, that supreme need not to ever truly be vulnerable to anyone, rearing up inside of him.

He tried to push all thought away, except the fact that at the moment, she was still here, and she was in his arms. He thought about how small and vulnerable she was, about the fine trembling running through her body, the sweet smell of her hair and the way it felt when he slipped his fingers into it at her nape, to cup her head and hold her face pressed against his chest.

Breathing as slowly and easily as he could manage— because even that still hurt—he dug deep for the patience not to push her, not to rush her, not to mess this up.

Finally, in a small, shaky voice, she admitted, "Honestly, James, I can't think of anything you could say about the last night we were together that would make any difference."

He winced at that, knowing it was only what he deserved. "Let me say it anyway, please? Decide for yourself if it makes a difference, and then if you still want to go…"

Damn, he couldn't even say it. That she could go anytime she wanted to, that this chance for them together could disappear at any time.

"I can't make you stay," he finally settled for saying. "I never could."

"This is ridiculous," she said, pushing gently against his chest, careful of his bruises but insistent as she stepped away from him. "You're exhausted."

He thought she was going to leave then, but instead, he felt her hands on the waistband of his slacks, undoing the top clasp and then matter-of-factly drawing down the zipper.

At her touch, he sucked in a breath, which hurt, dammit, and just stood there while she slid his slacks over his hips and let them drop to the floor.

"Sit," she said.

He put a hand on the headboard to brace himself and eased down to sit on the edge of the mattress. The soreness in his abused muscles was definitely setting in, as the doctor had warned.

She knelt at his feet and slid his shoes off, followed by his socks and slacks. Then she stood up, holding the sheet and comforter out for him as she ordered, "In the bed."

It took a moment but he complied, easing farther onto the mattress and then getting his legs onto the bed. She fluffed up pillows and stacked them behind his head and back, propping him up at an angle as the doctor had suggested.

Finally satisfied, she helped him ease back onto the pillows and asked, "Better?"

"Yes, thank you."

"I left your pain pills in my purse on the hall table. I'll go get them—"

He stopped her with a hand on her arm. "I don't want them."

"Don't be such a stupid man about it. You're hurting. Take the pills."

"If I can't sleep, I will. I promise." But they were strong and made him fuzzy-headed. At least, he thought it was the pills doing that to him today. If he could get her to listen to him about their breakup, he'd need a clear head.

"You are so stubborn," she complained.

He laughed. "And you're not?"

And then they both fell silent.

She'd jumped up to go get his pills, and now she stood there, uncertain and clearly warring with herself about what to do next, looking as tired and vulnerable as could be.

Still, he held out his hand to her, which she took, and told her, "Just curl up on the bed with me, and let me hold you. I'm not sure if I could manage any more than that tonight."

She looked truly annoyed with him at first. Sweet, worried about him, but annoyed. And when he watched very, very closely, he would swear she was swaying slightly on her feet, toward him and then away from him, as if the need to be closer to him was warring with an equally strong desire to get away.

He waited, honestly thinking she was going to leave, braced for it, telling himself not to beg, when she finally asked, "I don't suppose you've acquired a pair of pajamas since the last time I was here?"

"No," he said carefully. Did that mean she was staying?

"T-shirts still in the same place?" she asked.

He nodded, closing his eyes, honestly not sure if he could have gotten any words out at that moment. He had these white, cotton undershirts he wore under dress shirts in the winter, when it got cold, and she liked to sleep in them. They were the simplest things, short-sleeved with a little V in the neck, hitting her at about midthigh. He'd watch her so many times, her hair loose and free and a little bit wild, her face scrubbed clean, wearing nothing but one of his shirts and looking sexy as hell as she walked over to the bed to climb into it with him.

He heard footsteps, drawers opening and closing, and then a moment later, when he opened his eyes, there she was, backlit for just a moment by the soft light coming from the bathroom, looking even more beautiful than the image he'd been able to conjure up in his mind.

She flicked off the light and became nothing but a shadowy image, walking across the floor and sliding into his bed, not nearly as close as he'd like her to be. It was a damned big bed, something he regretted right that minute.

She leaned over, kissed him on the cheek and said, "Go to sleep." Then she rolled onto her side, facing away from him.

Okay.

He could work with that.

He eased onto his side, slowly and carefully fitting the front of his body to the back of hers from head to toe, nerve endings coming alive, humming with happiness, lush expanses of naked and nearly naked skin against naked skin.

One of his arms slid beneath her head as a pillow for her and one went around her waist. He groaned, letting the weight of his body sink against hers, tucking that perfect little bottom against his groin, sliding his hand beneath her T-shirt and onto the bare skin of her stomach.

There, that was perfect.

He sighed in pure contentment now that he was close enough that he could bury his nose in her hair and inhale that perfect Chloe scent of hers. And despite all he'd been through, he was getting hard from wanting her.

"Not as worn-out as you thought?" she asked.

"Apparently not," he said, grinning for all he was worth, letting his hand slide lower on her belly, using it to press her bottom more firmly against him. She wasn't wearing any panties, and it was heaven and hell at the same time.

And if he wasn't completely out of his mind, he'd swear that she was pressing that perfect bottom against him ever so slightly.

He turned his face into her hair, kissing her shoulder, slowly, softly, giving her time to object if she wanted to. When she didn't, he kissed his way down to her neck. Chloe loved it when he nibbled on her neck.

She shivered and started rocking her bottom against him, the pressure exquisite and absolutely perfect.

Finally, she rolled over in his arms, looked him in the eye and said, "You're supposed to rest, remember? To not exert yourself."

"Then be gentle with me," he said.

She looked like she wanted to smack him.

He grinned. "You can do as much or as little as you want. I will have no complaints."

Taking a breath, she tentatively touched her lips to his, like she didn't trust herself to really kiss him yet. Her hands on his chest were trembling, as was his whole body.

"You rat," she said. "You tricked me, Mr. Too Weak To Try Anything."

"I haven't done anything yet," he said as his hands slid beneath the hem of her shirt to cup her bare bottom, which felt every bit as perfect as he remembered.

"You got me into bed with you," she reminded him.

He grinned. "Yes, I did."

"You even got me to take your clothes off of you."

"Wasn't even trying for that, although it was a nice surprise."

She sighed and pouted a little, looking adorable. He wanted her. Finally, she kissed him, fiercely and yet with a gentleness that just broke his heart. There were tears seeping out of her eyes, and he thought she was still a little bit mad at him for scaring her at the hospital and maybe now for making her want him again.

After a long moment, she pushed him gently onto his back and threatened him. "Don't you dare let me hurt you."

Then she peeled off her shirt, grabbed a foil packet from the nightstand drawer, which she handed to him, and then helped him out of his briefs, putting the condom on him herself.

She sat up, braced her hands carefully on his shoulders and shifted to straddle his hips, draping her beautiful, naked body over him with extreme care. It was an all-over Chloe caress.

He groaned, his hands clenching on her hips, rubbing her body against his, and she let him, helped him along, moving in time with the push and pull of his hands. Her breasts nestled against his chest, and her lips settled onto his, and suddenly, the world was a beautiful and perfect place.

She kissed him for a long time, so softly, so sweetly, until he nearly lost his mind. Finally, she raised her hips, arched her back ever so slightly and then took him slowly, carefully inside of her, her body pulsing, easing, working to make room, to let him in.

All the air came out of him in a rush, and then he drew in a deep breath that hurt, but he didn't care, because there was the most exquisite sense of wholeness to the moment, of coming home. To her.

His hands pressed hard against her hips, halting their movement.

"Does it hurt?" she asked, going absolutely still.

"No, just give me a minute," he said through clenched teeth. His body was throbbing away inside of hers. "I just need to feel…everything, and I don't want it to ever stop. I know that's impossible, but I just need it so much."

She nuzzled her cheek against his, kissing him ever so softly, holding his face between her hands, trying to stay still, to give him time.

"I've missed you like crazy," he confessed. "There were times when I was convinced I'd never have you like this again, and that I'd regret that every day of my life."

Her eyes came open, her gaze locking on his as he got the last part out, her look part hurt and part mad.

"Believe me?" he asked.

And she looked away.

He swore softly, and then while he was still trying to figure out what else he could say to her, she started rocking her body against his until he couldn't think of anything else but what was happening between them in that moment. He felt everything so intensely, need, regret, hurt, anger, sadness, love….

He loved her. He did.

He couldn't deny it any longer. He wanted a hell of a lot more than her back in his bed, glorious as that was.

She came in a long, drawn-out clenching of her body around his, going completely boneless in his arms when it was over.

He groaned, held her hard against him for a moment, then another, and then, there came that perfect point in time when the whole world fell away, dissolving into pure sensation alone, when nothing mattered except the two of them, and how they made each other feel.

The world was perfect.

Everything was.

She was his again.

* * *

Chloe didn't regret it.

Not exactly.

She'd missed him too much to regret it completely. But she really wasn't ready for this, either, because she didn't really trust him. And what kind of woman went to bed with a man she didn't really trust?

A stupid one.

Still, she let him hold her in the dark cave of his bedroom, let him stroke those big, hot hands of his lazily over her body as he kept trying to get comfortable during what was a restless sleep at best.

And when she finally felt bad enough about what she'd allowed to happen, she got up, slipped on his T-shirt and headed for the kitchen.

"Where are you going?" he asked softly, before she'd even made it out of the room.

"To get your pain pills, so you can get some sleep." And she could run away and hide in her attic at her house and think about what she'd let herself do with him. She was back a moment later with the pills and some water, hoping she looked every bit as stubborn as he did at the moment. "You're taking these. You promised you would, if you need them. And you obviously need them."

"You promised we'd talk, too."

"Now?" She sat down on the side of the bed, facing him. "James, it's the middle of the night."

"So? You're here. I'm here. We're both awake. We've avoided it long enough, don't you think? Besides, you promised."

"You promised, too. You said you'd take your pain pills and get some rest."

"Fine. I take those, you and I talk. Now. Before they

make me feel like I've got cotton balls for brains and can't think," he offered.

It was a terrible bargain. No bargain at all. She felt ridiculous and cowardly and…scared. Scared of what he was going to say.

He held out his hands for the pills and the glass of water, and she gave them to him. Could she stall until they took effect, and he fell asleep? She wanted to.

He swallowed them and gave her back the empty glass, which she put on the nightstand. "James, I'm tired. I know you're tired, too. Can't we just—"

"It's the biggest issue standing between us, Chloe, and you won't even let me say how sorry I am or how terrible I feel about it. Why won't you let me even tell you about that last night?"

Oh, she hated this. Absolutely hated it. Hiding from the past was so much easier. "Because…it doesn't really matter anymore—"

He scoffed at that. "Oh, it matters. How can you even say that?"

"I mean, it doesn't matter because…I just have to forget about it. I have to move past it, because I want to be with you now, and I can't do that if I'm still holding on to everything that went wrong between us before. So there's just no point in reliving it all anyway, when I know what I have to do—"

He stared at her, and she watched the carious emotions flickering across his face. From trying and trying to figure out exactly what she was saying, what was behind the words, to hurt and finally to out-and-out fury.

"You think I'm going to lie to you again?" he asked incredulously.

She shook her head. "I…I just—"

"Oh, my God, you do! Even now, that's what you think

of me. That I'm just another in a long string of damned lying men."

"No. I just…I can't imagine anything you could say that would really make it better."

"You thought I'd lie," he insisted.

"I just didn't…want to know. I thought we could just… never talk about it, and after a while, it really wouldn't matter anymore. Because I don't want that to stand in our way of being together now. I don't want anything to take that away from us."

"We don't stand a chance of any kind of lasting relationship if you don't trust me." He took her by the arms and pulled her to him. "Look at me, Chloe. Look at me."

She finally did.

He was furious. Why was he so mad? She was the one who had the right to be mad.

"Ask me what happened," he ordered her.

She shook her head.

"Ask me!"

"I know what happened," she told him.

"Do you? Do you really know? Are you absolutely sure I'm as guilty as you think I am? Ask me!"

She cringed at the quiet fury in his voice. "Fine. What happened?"

He took a breath, winced because it obviously hurt him to do so and then began. "We had an awful fight that day."

Chloe nodded. She remembered it well.

"It seemed like we'd been doing nothing but fighting about one thing or another for weeks," he said.

Her business. The money he'd invested. The way she felt as if he was taking over, that she was losing control of both the business and her life to him. And the other women. There seemed to always be women throwing themselves at him, one more persistent than all the others. A model

Chloe knew named Giselle, someone she'd never liked and a woman who'd never liked Chloe, all over some supposed slight to Giselle in a show Chloe had done years ago when they were both starting out.

"We went to that party, and Giselle was there," he said.

Chloe had wanted to leave on the spot. She didn't think she could take any more, that she could see that woman and not be half-insane with jealousy over what she feared James had been doing with her.

"You and I argued again there," he said. Chloe nodded. She remembered.

"I ended up on the terrace, and there was Giselle, following me. And I was mad, Chloe. I was so tired and angry, and I just… What did you say to me just a few minutes ago? I just didn't think there was anything left that I could say to you to change things, to make you believe me. That I hadn't been sleeping with her behind your back all along. Even though I hadn't."

Chloe winced. "James—"

"The only times I'd put my hands on the woman were to push her away. I won't say she didn't try. She did. But I—"

"You didn't push her away that night. I saw you, dammit! I was there. I know what I saw," she cried.

"I know you were there. I knew it all along. I have a kind of radar where you're concerned, Chloe. My whole body goes on alert. I knew you were there," he insisted. "And I also knew that I was making you miserable and that you didn't trust me, and I thought to myself, why was I still even trying to make it work between us? And I just gave up."

He took in a ragged breath and let it out slowly.

"What you saw was me giving up on us," he said. "Right then and there."

"No," she said.

"I gave up on the idea that I could ever get you to trust me to be faithful to you or to stay with you. That we could make our relationship work. That I could make you happy." He shook his head. "You saw me giving up, and there she was. I knew if you saw us together, we'd be over, right then. No more fighting, no more trying, no more feeling lousy for not being able to make it work. Just over. So I did it. I kissed her, and I made sure you saw it."

Chloe could see it. She hurt more right then than she thought she had on the terrace that night, watching him with Giselle in his arms. He'd looked up at one point, seen Chloe standing there and gone right back to kissing Giselle.

Chloe had wanted to claw the woman's eyes out, right there on the spot, but hurt soon overrode anger, and she'd simply turned around and left instead.

"I'm sorry," James said. "I'm so sorry. I didn't realize until it was too late, what I was throwing away."

"You two were together for weeks afterward," Chloe remembered.

"I know," he admitted. "She wasn't you. And if I wasn't going to be with you, it really didn't matter to me who I was with."

Chloe squeezed her eyes shut, wishing it was as easy to shut the image out of her mind of the two of them together. "I saw pictures of the two of you together for a while. It was awful."

"And you were engaged six months later," he said. "I wanted to come find the man and tear him limb from limb. I still do."

Chloe let her tears fall onto his shoulder, felt him drop a little kiss on her forehead. "I'm not saying I was a good guy. I'm saying I wasn't the rat you thought I was, who'd been cheating on you all along, and I hope to God you can believe that and that it makes a difference to you. And that you believe me when I say I know what I gave up when I walked away from you, and I've regretted it practically every minute of my life since then."

"I missed you, too," she admitted. "So much."

"So, that's it. That's what I wanted to tell you. I hope you believe me, although I'm not sure you will, even now, and it scares the hell out of me."

To which she said nothing, just let him hold her against him. And when he finally fell into a deep sleep, she got up, got dressed and, like a complete coward, ran out of there.

Chapter Ten

Chloe slipped in the back entrance to her house, not seeing any actual riots out front at that hour. But inside, once she'd showered and dressed, she was confronted with the evidence of what had happened in the days since the infamous runway brawl.

Dresses. Her beautiful dresses. Ones she'd poured her heart and soul into, rejected by superstitious brides and left in a heap in the storage room. Poor, sad, abandoned dresses. She sat there with them, feeling like she should apologize for all those broken dreams. At some point, she must have fallen back to sleep.

Addie found her there, hours later, hidden away with the poor, rejected gowns. "Okay, this is not good for any of us."

"Do you think they'll go on with their weddings? All these brides who brought their dresses back?" Chloe asked.

"I don't know," Addie said, looking truly worried about Chloe.

"Because I love our brides, and I want them to be happy, even if we can't be. I hope they all find another dress and go right on. I'd hate it if my lousy luck in love was enough to put them over the edge, too."

"Over the edge? Chloe, what—"

"You know, like you're trying to hang on, you're trying to believe, but you're really scared and one more bad thing is enough to make you just throw up your hands and give up. I feel like anybody getting married these days has to be barely hanging on, barely keeping all that fear at bay. I mean, who really believes in love anymore?"

"Dammit, you slept with him, didn't you?" Addie cried.

"Yes, I did."

"Battered, bruised, concussed, and the man can still get you into bed with him? Amazing."

"He is amazing," she admitted. There was no denying it. "Infuriating and frustrating. Sneaky, scary and amazing."

"Okay, so you had great sex with him—"

"We didn't have great sex—"

"Oh, come on. You don't look like a woman who had bad sex. I hate him, and even I don't think a woman could have bad sex with him."

"We didn't have bad sex, either. We had…sad, needy, overwhelming sex. I wouldn't let him move. No, I barely let him move, and there was nothing to it because I was trying not to hurt him and yet, I just had to be with him. There's nothing we did that should have felt that good, that amazing, but it did, because…it was him. That's all I need for it to be amazing. Just him." She stopped to take a breath, to look over at her sister. "And, at the same time, I still don't trust him."

Addie honestly looked like she was at a loss for words, which happened maybe once in a decade.

"In my own defense," Chloe said, "I did realize how wrong it was, and once he fell asleep, I got up and ran out of there."

"Too late." Addie shook her head. "Way too late. And this is the first place he's going to come looking for you when he wakes up."

"I know. We talked about Giselle. I finally let him talk about it." She went through the whole thing with Addie.

"So, do you believe him?" she asked when Chloe was done.

"I want to. And I think, too, how much of what happened back then, what I felt, what I thought was happening, was about him and anything he was doing, and how much of it was me and all my insecurities about relationships? Me thinking like I always have. 'What would a man like him be doing with someone like me? Why would I ever believe any man could be faithful or that any relationship could last?' I mean, did I give him a fair chance before the whole Giselle thing? Do I give any man a fair chance? I'm not sure I ever have."

"No, we never have," Addie conceded.

"The end was coming for me and James. I knew that before I saw him with Giselle that night. It was coming because we didn't trust each other. If he'd never done a single thing to deserve my doubts, I still wouldn't have trusted him. Not because of who he was. Because of who I was. I'm no good at this."

"Yeah, there is the whole family curse thing." Addie shrugged, shook her head. "And I hate to admit it—you know how much I hate this—but I can see how a man would decide to end a relationship by doing something like making sure you saw him with someone else. I can see a man thinking that was a chance to end things quickly, once and for all, and taking it."

"I hurt him, Addie. I mean, he hurt me. You know how much he did."

Addie nodded, giving Chloe a little hug.

"But I hurt him, too. I believe that. I believe he regrets the way he hurt me, the way he ended things."

"You just still don't know if he was faithful to you until the night you saw him and Giselle together."

Chloe groaned and buried her head in her hands, "I know. Believe me, I know. That's why I left. So I could try to figure it out."

"And you haven't yet?"

"No, not yet."

"Well, I hate to add to your misery—especially with this, and please know, I'm embarrassed that it ever came to this. But you have to talk to James, because that idiot Marcy has really lost it this time, and she has a plan to try to save her job and explain away the whole photo/jail/fight thing between me and her that doesn't involve either of us sleeping with James."

"What's so bad about that?" Chloe asked.

"Her explanation is that Marcy and I are both crazy in love with the security guard, Wayne, and we're both having his alien baby."

"Alien baby?" That had to be some kind of sick joke.

"Marcy says to the tabloids, nothing beats an alien-baby story, and she's been devouring them since she was nine. So Wayne's supposedly from another planet, and we're both having his alien baby."

Chloe just shook her head. "I don't think there's anything I could possibly say to that."

"Apparently, even alien men can't be trusted to sleep with only one woman at a time. I'm cynical enough to believe that. And you were upset in that photo outside the jail because…I mean, you would be upset to find out your sister was being two-timed by an alien, wouldn't you?"

"No one is ever going to believe a word of that—"

Addie shrugged, looking resigned to their collective fate. "I figure if it's too late, and she's already put out the story, you could issue a statement saying that naturally, you'll love your half-alien niece or nephew, because…you know…everybody needs and deserves love. No judgments here. Just love."

"We're doomed," Chloe said. "That's all there is to it. We're doomed."

"Yeah, probably, we are." Addie looked sad and worried and a little bit mad. "And if that wasn't enough to make your day, there's someone outside who insists on seeing you. I was going to try to deal with him myself, but…right now, I think I'll leave that up to you."

"Who?"

"You're going to have to see for yourself to believe it. He's out front. Robbie tried to get him someplace less conspicuous but he wouldn't budge."

Chloe couldn't imagine who was waiting for her, but decided if it wasn't James, she could handle it. Bracing herself, she went into the showroom.

Robbie was there, looking truly astonished and pointing to the front doors. "I begged him to leave, but that's as far as I could get him."

Begged? Who did he have to beg to leave?

She opened the big front door and walked out onto the porch and saw Bryce pacing back and forth.

Chloe just stood there with her mouth hanging open.

Bryce?

"Chloe!" he cried, rushing to her side.

He still had a bandage on the side of one eye, but otherwise he looked fine. Not scarred for life, it seemed.

"What in the world are you doing here?" she asked.

"I just had to see you." He grabbed her by the arms and positively beamed at her. "Chloe, I am so, so sorry. For everything. I never meant to hurt you. Please believe that."

Chloe wanted to point out that given the fact that they had been engaged and he'd been cheating on her with another man, she was bound to end up hurt, but she just didn't have the energy for that whole conversation.

"Bryce, what do you want?"

"To see you. To tell you how sorry I am, Chloe."

"Okay, you've said it."

Still, he just stood there, holding on to her and, if she wasn't seriously mistaken, looking like…like he… Surely, he didn't want…

And then he pulled her against him and kissed her. She was too shocked to stop him, and when she didn't make any response at all, he finally stopped.

"Chloe, I'm done with Reginald."

"Who?"

"You know, Eloise's boyfriend. It was a huge mistake right from the beginning. I don't think I realized how much we had until it was gone. I miss you, Chloe, and I want you back."

"You're insane," she said.

"No, I'm not. That story about me in the mental hospital was all a lie. You know how those tabloids make up things." He frowned then. "Although I have to say, I hope the latest one about James…I kind of hope that one's true."

"No, it's not. James is not sleeping with Addie or his assistant."

"Not that story. The one that said you left him over it, and he was so upset, he's on suicide watch after trying to kill himself by walking into traffic yesterday."

Chloe groaned out loud. It was all she could do not to scream.

"Yeah, I know, that's not very nice of me, to hope he's in such bad shape," Bryce said, looking a bit sheepish. "I really wasn't hoping he was suicidal, just that he was sleeping around, too, and you were done with him. And that you might take me back. I mean, you gave him a second chance. You're a kind, generous woman. Give me another chance, too. I won't blow it, I swear."

"I don't believe this," Chloe said. "I just honestly can't believe it."

"Please, just think about it. Let me see you every now and then. I need you, Chloe. We were good together."

God must hate her, Chloe decided. God, the universe, every living entity must hate her and be in on a plot to torment her right now for some reason she could not understand.

"Bryce, you lied to me, over and over again. You slept with another model in the show, and because the whole thing came out in that hideously public way, my life as a designer is probably ruined. I'm probably going to lose everything. So, no, I'm not going to give you another chance."

He looked shocked at that.

How could he possibly be shocked?

Then he reached for her again, and just as he got his hands on her, she heard an absolute growl of outrage from behind her.

James had been absolutely furious when he woke up and she was gone.

No note. No explanation. Nothing. He shouldn't have laid a hand on her the night before, shouldn't have pushed. He knew that. He'd just missed her so damned much, wanted her so much, and it was more his fault than hers that she'd run out on him. But he was still mad. Especially because she'd finally let him tell her about what really happened between him and Giselle, but hadn't said a word about whether she believed him or not. And then, she ran out on him, which he thought was probably a bad sign.

He'd calmed down a little bit by the time he got to the street in front of her shop, but then he looked up and saw...

Chloe kissing another man!

He felt like he was hit by the bike messenger again, taking a blow to the chest, to his already-bruised heart. He couldn't move at first, couldn't so much as speak.

Chloe was kissing another man!

James wanted to kill him, right there on the spot. She'd crawled out of his bed sometime last night or early this morning and run home to kiss another man!

Deciding not to kill first and ask questions later, he walked slowly and deliberately toward them. They were done kissing, and were now talking. He couldn't see Chloe's face, but from what he could see of the guy's, he looked the way James imagined he had with Chloe lately—desperate to make her understand something he was trying to tell her. Maybe it was wishful thinking on James's part, but he didn't think the guy was having any more luck with that than James had.

Then the jerk reached for her again to kiss her.

No way James was going to stand by and watch that happen again.

He lunged forward, got himself between the two of them and shoved the guy back with all his might. Chloe gasped. The guy looked confused, scared and somehow familiar. James might have actually growled. He couldn't be sure.

Then he got up in the guy's face and snarled, "You touch her again and it'll be the last friggin' thing you do—"

"James?" Chloe said, tugging on his arm, trying to get him to back off. "What are you doing?"

He didn't turn to face her. He wanted to see the look on this guy's face when he said, "I woke up this morning and was surprised you weren't still there in bed with me, Chloe."

She growled herself. "James, honestly—"

Her guy looked mad and more than a little scared. "Wait, this is James? The guy who's supposed to be suicidal over you? Yeah, I saw him in the tabloids. You're really seeing him again?"

"Yes, she is!" James was definitely growling in outrage. No other word quite fit the sounds coming out of his mouth.

Chloe got herself between the two of them, looked at James and yelled, "Shut up!"

Then she turned her back to him and faced his rival. "Bryce, leave now. Leave right now—"

He looked like he was going to pout. "Are you at least going to think about getting back together with me?"

"What?" *Get back together?* Wasn't he seeing one of Chloe's male models?

"No, I'm not. I have other men to torment me, to break my heart and help prove to the world that I am, indeed, cursed in love. Your part is done. You can go now."

He started to argue. But James loomed over her shoulder, trying to look as mean and scary as he could while Chloe held him back. After a moment, Bryce seemed to get the message.

They stood there together watching him leave, and then Chloe turned and faced James looking mad as hell.

"Nice caveman act," she said.

"I'm not acting. I saw him kiss you, and I wanted to kill

him right there on the spot. What's he doing here, any-way?"

"Apparently he wants me back."

James was truly baffled. Her ex-secretly-gay-fiancé wanted her back? "Why?"

Chloe was fuming then. "I don't know. My sparkling personality, maybe? My ability to bring chaos into the lives of everyone around me? My failing business? I have so much to offer, you know?"

"Okay, you know I didn't mean it like that. I meant… the guy was sleeping with another one of the models at your show. He ruined everything for you. How could he think you'd take him back after that?"

"Funny you should ask. He said he read in the tab-loids that I'd decided to give you another chance—despite knowing how things ended between you and me—and he thought, what the hell, cheater or not, maybe I'd give him another chance, too."

James felt like he could breathe fire at that, he was so damned mad. Mad at her for running away this morning. Mad at that other guy who'd dared touch her, who'd been engaged to her. Mad at the world for what had happened to her business, her dream. But mostly mad at himself for giving up on the two of them a year and a half ago and bringing them to this point.

"Chloe, please," he began, but before he could say more, Addie stepped between them and whispered fiercely.

"This may not matter anymore. We may have given up completely on saving ourselves," she said, "but you have at least one audience member with a camera pointed at you. I thought I should at least ask if you'd like to go upstairs and fight."

In James's mind, the words *given up completely on sav-*

ing ourselves hit, and hit hard. Who the hell was giving up? And why?

They couldn't give up. If they did, Chloe had no reason to see him again, nothing he could use to push her into seeing him, and he felt like a man who really needed a reason for her to see him right now.

"I would love to go upstairs," James said, as calmly as possible.

And once he got inside, he'd just refuse to leave.

Chloe gave him a wide berth in the house and even on the way upstairs to her bedroom. She didn't want to be anywhere near a bed with him, but her room was the most private place in the house.

He stood in front of the only chair in her room, waiting, looking positively grim and still very, very angry.

Chloe couldn't say she minded the angry part that much. He deserved to feel bad after the way things had ended with them before. And she had to admit, it was a little flattering, thinking he was so jealous of her and any man that he could hardly get words out. Still, jealous of Bryce? Did he seriously think there was any way in the world she'd get back together with Bryce?

"Could I sit down, please?" he asked.

She nodded, watching him as he did. He had a black eye. He looked like he was hurting a lot more today than he had been yesterday, and she began to feel the urge to cut him some slack because of that. She sat next to him on her bed and faced him, trying to figure out what she wanted to say. Things were just so crazy. She didn't know where to start. Apparently, he did.

"What did Addie mean about giving up on saving your business?"

Chloe blinked up at him. "That's what you want to talk about right now? Business?"

He threw his hands up in the air. "I want to talk about a lot of things. This is just a place to start."

"A place to start?" she repeated.

"Yes. Can we start there, please? You love what you do. I know you do. You can't give up on saving your career."

"Everything we've tried to do has only made things worse. Apparently, we're just really bad at pretense. Do you even know how ridiculous it's gotten? Yesterday, while you and I were at the hospital, Marcy wanted to try to make people believe that she and Addie weren't sleeping with you, they were both sleeping with Wayne, the security guard, instead—"

"What's so bad about that?"

"And that Wayne's an alien, and that she and Addie are both having his alien babies!"

"Alien babies? Okay, yeah. That's bad—"

"Yeah," Chloe insisted. "There's no coming back from the double-alien-baby claim. We can only hope it's not already too late to stop her, because otherwise, we'd have absolutely no credibility about anything. People would either think we're lunatics or liars. So if you want to do something, go find Marcy and make sure she doesn't say anything else to anyone about aliens. Honestly, even without that, things seem pretty hopeless."

James seemed to take that particularly hard. He looked like a man in serious pain. She was starting to really worry about him.

"Are you okay?" she asked finally.

"No. I said I was going to help you, and I've done nothing but make things worse—"

"Oh, that reminds me, in case you haven't heard yet, you're supposed to be so upset over how I've treated you, that you deliberately walked into traffic yesterday and now you're on suicide watch in a Manhattan mental hospital. I've driven another man to the brink of suicide."

"Oh, no," he groaned.

"Yes. The whole Chloe-cursed-in-love thing is going full steam again. Brides are still freaked, and we're doomed."

"We are not doomed," he insisted. "Although, obviously, it's going to take something truly drastic to overcome this."

"Drastic? You got run over. There's nothing more drastic than that," she explained.

"It doesn't have to be something bad," he said. "It could be something good, something happy."

"We've been trying to pull off happy, and it's all turned out awful."

"Chloe, I think we have to get married." He paled a little as he said it, but looked determined.

She just stared at him at first.

Married?

Then she laughed a bit, because… Another man claiming he wanted to marry her? That was where all her troubles started, and the idea of getting engaged for a fourth time… There was something really pathetic about that, especially when she'd never yet made it to the altar.

"No. I am never getting engaged again—"

"I didn't say anything about being engaged. I said married."

"Well, I can't get married without getting engaged—"

"Of course you can. Skip the whole engagement part. Maybe that's the problem. Go straight to the marriage part."

"That's insane," she insisted.

His face turned grim, looking positively bloodless for

a moment. She thought he might collapse right there. But he rallied.

"First rule of disaster PR. Change the story. A wedding is a great, happy story and the only way I see to kill the whole notion of a curse."

She shot him an incredulous look. "You can't be serious."

James watched her and waited, looking more concerned with each passing moment. Finally, he said, "It doesn't have to be a real wedding. We can just make it look real. We'll go to city hall for a license, book a church, get you an engagement ring."

She shook her head, hurt, scared and so tired. Were they trying to save her business or starting a new relationship? Last night, it had felt like they were starting over, even though she still had issues—rightly so—about trusting him. Now he was acting as if this was all one big farce, and he was playing right along.

"Look, it's been a crazy week or so. I'm exhausted. I can't think about anything right now," she said.

He looked truly alarmed. "It's a good plan. It will work."

"It just sounds like more of what we've already tried."

He looked as if she'd stabbed him through the heart or something.

She got scared again. "James, are you sure you're feeling all right this morning?"

"I'm fine," he insisted. "But we don't have much time to turn this around—"

She groaned, feeling so weary. "I just want some time to think."

"Fine. I can be quiet," he insisted. "I'll stay right here, and I won't say a word—"

"No," she said, watching his jaw tighten as she said it, then tried to say it in a nicer way. "Please. I want you to go."

Chloe lay in her bed and cried for a while after he left, feeling like she deserved the indulgence of a few tears after the horrors of the last thirty hours or so. After about an hour, Robbie came in and handed her the tabloid claiming James was suicidal over her. He quickly left her alone.

She hardly glanced at the story. It was the photo of him lying on the street bleeding that grabbed her attention, that she couldn't get out of her mind. He'd been hit by that newsstand just down the street from his apartment, where he bought a newspaper every morning. She'd been there with him before.

So what had really happened yesterday? She'd bet he'd walked up to the newsstand, seen the tabloid with the claims of their foursome with Addie and Marcy and been so distracted he'd stepped in front of the bike messenger and nearly gotten himself killed.

It was too horrible for words.

She'd nearly gotten him killed, sat by his side in the E.R. that day and then ended up in his bed that night. Making love to him had been like ripping her soul wide open. And what had he suggested this morning? More pretense.

She was sick of the games. She was done. Whatever happened from here on out would just happen. No more lies.

Soon Addie knocked tentatively and opened the door to peek in. "Sorry. I know I hardly ever say anything else to you and it is a cliché at this point, a bad one, but…we have a problem."

Chloe sighed. "Tell me it's not Bryce again."

"No," Addie said. "Does he really want you back?"

Chloe nodded. "Please don't tell me how ridiculous that is or ask me any questions. I can't deal with that right now."

"You know, I'm going to make you some of that tea for PMS. It really takes me down a notch when I need it, and right now you need it."

"I need a whole lot more than PMS tea, believe me. Now, what's my new problem?"

"James. What happened with him earlier?"

"He came up with a new plan to save the business."

Addie looked puzzled. "We need a new plan to save the business. What's so bad about his plan?"

"It involves me marrying him," she said, trying to keep from showing just how much that hurt—to have him offer to marry her to save her business. Not because he loved her.

"You're kidding. He really wants to marry you?"

"Of course not. He wants to fake marry me. He doesn't do things for real. He doesn't know how," Chloe cried. "Okay, for a few hours last night, he knew how. He did. He just got it, the whole thing, so real it probably scared him half to death. Me, too. And now, we're back to fake courtship, fake love, fake marriage. No man will ever want to do more than fake marry me."

Addie paused, looking concerned. "You're right. This is a job for way more than PMS tea. I still can't believe he wants to marry you. To even pretend to marry you—"

"Gee, thanks, Addie. I feel so much better now."

"Oh, you know what I mean. Men like him…they get the willies even mentioning the marriage thing, let alone ever actually getting close to it."

"He asked me to marry him before for real. We were engaged! For real! At least, I thought it was real."

"Yeah, but neither one of you ever actually did anything to move toward a wedding date."

"Okay, you're right. You got us there. Maybe it never would have happened. Maybe I'm doomed. No, cursed. I forgot. What I am is cursed."

"You're kind of scaring me today," Addie said.

"I'm scaring myself today. I scared myself half to death last night, and he scared me half to death yesterday. If he'd bounced the other way after the biker hit him, he'd probably have been hit by a car and be dead now, and it would be my fault. After all the things we've done to try to save my business. And I am not doing it anymore. I'm done. Whatever happens to the business happens."

"Well, if that's how you really feel—"

"I'm sorry. I'm so sorry. Especially about letting you and Robbie and Connie down—"

"Don't think about us now. Because, as I said earlier, we have a problem. The reason I came up here? James is downstairs, standing across the street just staring at the house. He won't leave. I already went over there and tried my best, but he won't budge. He's starting to freak out the neighbors again. I tried to tell them he wasn't dangerous, but I'm still afraid someone will call the cops on him, and, as I now know, jail is not a fun place."

Chloe groaned. "I thought he'd left. I told him to go, and he acted like he was going."

"You're going to have to go talk to him. No matter what it takes, get him to leave."

Chapter Eleven

"So." James stood on the street corner across from Chloe's, talking to Adam, who'd agreed to meet James at Chloe's to try to talk some sense into him. "Have you ever done anything stupid because of a woman?"

"No," Adam said. "I'm the one man on earth who understands women completely. They make perfect sense to me. So I've never done anything stupid for one."

James frowned. "That is not helping. You said you'd try to help me."

"Well, ask me a real question at least," Adam said. "This is about Chloe, right?"

"Of course it's about Chloe. She's the only woman who makes me crazy."

"And the problem is?"

"She makes me crazy!"

"Well, yeah. I mean, that's just part of it, if you really love her," Adam said, like there was nothing unusual about that.

"That's…that's insane. Love equals crazy? What the hell kind of plan is that? You love someone, and it automatically makes you crazy?"

"If you're lucky enough to really love them, yeah. Because it means too much. It's too important then. It's everything. And that means, to all us control freaks out there, that we're not really in control anymore. That someone else has the power to make or break us, and that's what gets to us."

"I am not a control freak," James said.

Adam just laughed. "Seriously? You're going to waste your breath even saying that?"

James sighed, feeling truly ill. "I don't know how to do this. The Chloe thing. The love thing."

"Nobody really does," Adam claimed.

"Don't say that. Some people have to know. They're in love. They even manage to stay in love and stay married. I thought they just knew how to do it."

"I don't think so," Adam mused. "I think they just want it so badly, they get in there and fight and suffer and even though they're scared, they figure it out."

"I never thought of it that way," James said, then confessed, "I panicked earlier and asked Chloe to marry me."

"Why?" James asked.

"Because she wanted to give up on trying to save her business, and if she does that, I'm afraid she might not see me again."

"Oh." Adam frowned. "So what did she say to your proposal?"

"She kicked me out of her house."

"Not a good sign."

"No, it's not. I mean, what I actually asked is for her to fake marry me. I started with 'Marry me,' and when she laughed at that… Oh, God, she laughed."

He'd felt just how bruised his heart was in that moment.

"Hey, I'm sorry," Adam said.

"Yeah, anyway, when it looked like really marrying me was out, I said, 'Fake marry me.' But that didn't really go over any better."

Adam nodded, giving James a look that said, *Man, you are so screwed.*

"And I never even worked up the nerve to tell her that I'm into her business for a couple hundred grand, more if she goes under after I pay you off," James remembered. "That's not going to go well. I guess I could fake marry her without telling her about the money, but I can't marry her for real without telling her."

"And you really want to marry her?" Adam asked, still looking like he thought James was screwed.

"I just want her to…never, ever leave me, no matter what. I don't ever want to have to live without her. I want her in my house and in my bed and sitting across from me at dinner every night, and smiling and happy and loving me." James threw up his hands in defeat. "What do I do? How do I make that happen?"

"I think you have to tell her all that, just like you told me. Get the money part out fast, and then move on to everything else."

James grimaced. "I don't think there's any way she'd marry me for real. I was hoping she'd fake marry me, and then we'd have some time for her to get used to the idea, to see how good this could be. I'd show her there was nothing fake about a marriage between us."

Adam nodded sympathetically. "Well, I guess you could go that way."

"I'm pretty sure it's my only chance right now," James admitted.

"Hey, you saw the tabloid thing, right? Saying you're suicidal over Chloe?"

"No, but I heard something about it."

"You should know, I'm hearing things about that deal you're about to close with Davidson?"

"It's all but done. We're signing the papers this week."

Adam shook his head. "The man's seriously spooked. I think he's looking for another partner. A friend of mine saw him talking to Syd Greenberg today. They've done business together before."

James swore. Now this whole disaster with Chloe was screwing up his business?

"I know. Sorry," Adam said. "And that girl who works for you? Marcy? Please tell me you're not sleeping with her."

"No, and I'm not sleeping with Chloe's sister, either!"

"Okay. I just had to ask. Now go tell Chloe the truth."

James stood as tall and straight as he could, took a fortifying, if painful, breath and said, "Okay. I'm ready. I'm going in."

Chloe peeked out the front window, and there was James, standing across the street talking to Adam. Where had he come from? At least Adam could talk some sense into him. Maybe. She hoped so. But then Adam stayed where he was and James started walking across the street toward the house.

"Dammit," she muttered.

She thought about hiding. She used to hide from difficult things all the time as a kid. Why didn't grown-ups just hide more often?

But she waited too long, and then there he was, looking as reluctant to be there as she was to have him there. Maybe he wanted to hide, too, Chloe thought. It wasn't too late. Or he could just turn around and leave again without saying a word. She wouldn't object.

But he didn't leave.

Instead, he said, "You look like you're about to run away from me again. Or try to push me out of your life again—"

"I did not push you out of my life—"

"You damned well tried, not an hour ago. I should know. I was there."

Chloe fumed. He was mad at her? "You think you have some right to be here? Let me remind you that you just showed up here when my life was falling apart and said you wanted to help, that you had a plan, that it would work. And we have made a complete and utter disaster of it."

"I know! Don't you think I know that? I feel terrible, Chloe. I don't know how it happened. It all seemed so easy, and now, here we are, in a huge mess."

Yes, they were. And his big answer was a fake marriage to her? She was still reeling from that.

"James, I told you I just needed—"

"I have to tell you something," he said, looking way too serious for her peace of mind.

Nothing good ever came out of a conversation that started with the words *I have to tell you something.*

"You really don't," Chloe told him.

"I do," James said grimly. "Adam told me I had to."

Adam? What did Adam have to do with anything between her and James? Adam was just…James's friend, and someone who'd put a lot of money into Chloe's business.

Money?

"Is this about Adam's investment in my company?" she asked, afraid things were about to get a whole lot worse. One would think that wasn't possible, after all that had already happened. But Chloe had found things could always get worse.

"Yes," James said.

Chloe swore softly and took James by the hand, leading him to the storage room at the back of the house, because that's where she went to hide and to think sometimes. It had a door, and usually, if she was in there with the door closed, everyone left her alone.

They went inside, and she shut the door behind them, leaning against it both for support and to make extra sure no one came in. "Okay, talk," she said.

He took a breath and let it out on a sigh, looking very guilty. "I'm sorry. I'll say that first, because you might not give me a chance to say it later. I'm really sorry. I never wanted you to even know this, and if things had worked out the way I hoped, you never would have."

Chloe didn't understand. "This is about you? I thought it was about Adam?"

"It's about all of us. Chloe, when we broke up, you wanted me out of your business right away, and I did my best to make that happen. But a company in the fashion industry is a high-risk start-up, and the economy was already showing some troubling signs even then."

"But then you found Adam," she said.

"I did. He did it as a personal favor to me and because I made him certain promises about his investment."

She frowned. "I don't understand. What kind of promises?"

"He put up his money, became your investor, and if you'd gone on to turn a profit, the two of you would have gone on as partners, and I'd be no part of it. And you'd never know the rest. I honestly thought that would happen but—"

"But it didn't, and now, here we are. What did you promise Adam?"

"I guaranteed his losses."

"Which means…?"

"That if he ended up losing money on the deal, I'd pay him back whatever he invested. Look, no one else would put money into a start-up clothing designer. No one. I'm sorry because I know it's not what you wanted—to have anything else to do with me—but it was the only thing I could think of to do that would allow you to stay in business, so I did it."

Chloe crossed her arms and glared at him. "So, all this time, ever since Adam came along, you've been lying to me about my own business?"

"I guess you could put it that way. I mean, we weren't speaking to one another. We didn't see each other, until very recently. I really hoped it wouldn't even matter."

Oh, she was seething. "Okay, just to be absolutely clear, do you have any other secrets you need to tell me?"

He shrugged, looked one way, then the other. "I…don't know… Maybe."

Chloe groaned. "What do you mean, you don't know? You have to know."

"I'm not sure if it qualifies as a separate issue or just… details about the secret I've already told you," he claimed.

"I think at this point, you should confess all and let me decide. Spill it!"

"Okay…after the runway thing, the riot, you needed another infusion of cash to get through it, and Adam just didn't have it to give. I wrote him a check the day of the riot, and he turned around and wrote a bunch of checks to all those angry brides."

Chloe just looked at him, hurt and angry. "God, it never stops with you! You just charge in and take over—"

"You think I wanted to do that? After all the grief between us about me trying to take over your business the first time around? No way I wanted to do that—"

"But you did, didn't you?"

"You would have gone under that day, if I hadn't," he told her. "That's the only reason I did it."

"Well, maybe I should have gone under! And if I was going to, it was my decision to make. Did you ever think of that?"

"I did." He shook his head. "But more than anything, I just wanted to buy you some time to save everything. I really thought we could."

She laughed, because honestly, what else was there to do?

They had failed miserably, made things worse, even, which she would have thought wasn't possible, given how awful things had been to start with.

"So, that's everything? There's nothing else you've lied to me about?"

"Nothing else," he said grimly.

"Fine. Now it's my turn. I want you to know that I am absolutely and completely done with all your plans and schemes. I will not tell one more lie with you."

"Okay."

"I will not go on one more fake date with you. We will not have one more fake kiss or fake embrace. There will be no more fake neck-nuzzling or fake foot massages in a limousine. Nothing. Got it?"

"Fine," he said.

"And I am so not having a fake engagement to you, and I will never, ever, ever fake marry you!"

"Fine!" he said, gritting his teeth.

"Fine."

He understood. She was glad. So why were they both so mad? He looked like steam might pour out of his nostrils at any moment, and then he'd breathe a little fire and burn the whole place down.

Chloe was breathing hard herself, furious, too, and then just hurt, so very hurt. "I just can't pretend anymore. I can't stand one more fake thing in my life. It's a mess, a huge mess, and I'm going to deal with it. I'm going to do what I want, what I think is right. No more lies. It's all going to be real."

"Okay," he said.

"So...you should really go."

Because, if they were being real...she didn't know what was left, and obviously he didn't, either, because his response to the night they'd spent together was the offer to fake marry her, the jerk!

Chloe finally got through the absolute worst of her fury and found a world of hurt roaring in behind it. She felt as if she was the one with a giant bruise on her heart, not him.

She opened up the door of the storage room, shoved him out, then closed the door behind him, sank down to the floor and cried.

Chloe was still mad the next morning, though she felt a little bad when she saw that more of the tabloids had picked up on the idea that James was suicidal over her.

"Serves him right," Addie claimed in the kitchen that morning over coffee. "And really, the timing isn't bad for him to be taking a walk in traffic over you, because *New York Woman* is out today with its stupid bachelor list, and he's on it. Maybe this will cut down on the number of women coming after him—"

"Addie—"

"Well, he claims to hate that sort of thing."

"Not enough to want people to think he's ready to kill himself. I mean, surely there are easier ways to make yourself less attractive to women."

"With him, I'm not so sure about that. This might be

his only shot, if what he really wants is to keep from having women swarming around him."

Chloe grabbed a doughnut and started munching. This was a morning that required sugary, gooey carbs and lots of them, and the doughnuts were still warm. She might eat the whole box, especially if Addie kept this up.

"Who went out for doughnuts?" Chloe asked. "These are great."

"Adam brought them. We're going over some budget issues this morning," Addie said, making a face.

"Oh, perfect." Chloe hadn't been able to bring herself to tell Addie or anyone else about James's little deal with Adam yet. She still had that to look forward to.

Adam came in a moment later, carrying his laptop, which he put on the kitchen table, and a tabloid, which he put in front of Chloe. The headline blared Chloe Strikes Again: She's Made Another Man Want to Kill Himself.

Chloe felt a buzz of hysterical laughter bubbling up inside of her, which she managed to hold back, just barely, by taking another bite of her doughnut and gnawing on it.

"Might be a two-boxes-of-pastry kind of morning," Addie told Adam.

"I can go get more," he offered.

Chloe chewed harder. "Never in my life could I have envisioned my career as a designer ending like this. It's too bizarre for words."

"It's not over," Addie claimed.

"Oh, it's over. I told James yesterday, and I meant it. No more schemes. No more lies. No more pretense. No fake engagements, no fake marriages. Nothing."

"Well, that's good, I guess. I mean, given that we seem incapable of pulling off any of that," Addie reasoned. "And it means you don't have to see James anymore. I know that's good."

Yes, it was good. It had to be good, Chloe tried to tell herself. He was a liar, a manipulator, a man who got run over by a bike messenger for her, but the whole pretend romance had been his idea in the first place, so it served him right. Right?

"I'm going to get my laptop, and we can compare numbers, Adam," Addie said, getting up and heading for her office.

Chloe sat there, feeling guilty with Adam looking at her the way he was. She liked Adam. He was a nice guy. He'd just been caught up in a scheme James came up with, that was all.

He kept staring at her. Chloe felt guiltier and guiltier. Finally, she said, "What?"

"James didn't want a fake relationship with you, Chloe. He didn't want a fake engagement or a fake marriage. He didn't tell you that?"

"I…just…" She thought about it. She'd told him she didn't want any of that. But he'd most definitely suggested fake dating and a fake marriage. "It was all his idea. All the fake stuff."

"Well, it's not what he wanted. You should ask him about that. And don't worry. I'm sure he'll be able to save that multimillion-dollar deal with Davidson even if Davidson thinks he's mentally unstable over you. I mean, it's James. He always comes out on top, right?"

Chloe looked up warily. "He's got a big deal falling apart over this?"

Adam nodded. "Big one."

"Well, I am sorry for that."

Adam just waited, watching her, leaving her feeling more guilty with every passing second.

"What did James really want from me?" she finally asked.

"Why don't you go ask him?" Adam suggested.

Chloe went to James's office that afternoon and found Marcy packing her things and—oddly—not looking upset at doing it. She actually looked happy. That was truly weird.

Approaching cautiously, Chloe said, "Please tell me you didn't put out the double-alien-baby story, Marcy."

"Oh, no. Mr. Elliott said no way to that one." Marcy kept on packing.

"So, did he fire you?"

"No, he helped me see that I'm really not meant for a career in finance. Honestly, I don't think I ever really wanted it. But my father really wanted it for me, and I loved him so much. I tried hard to make it work. He and Mr. Elliott go back a long way. They've done a lot of business together over the years. I'm pretty sure that's the only reason I got this job in the first place. Or kept it this long," Marcy admitted. "But my father's been gone for over a year now, and I'm not doing this anymore."

"Oh. Sorry about your father, Marcy. What are you going to do now?"

Her whole face lit up. "Mr. Elliott knows someone who knows someone who works in television, who got me a job as an assistant on a TV show! I'm so excited!"

Chloe tried not to make a face. "A gossip show?"

"Yes! Can you believe it?" Marcy did a little happy dance. "On the condition that I never, ever tell them a single thing about you, Mr. Elliott, your company, Addie, the bike messenger, Wayne… You know, about anything." She made a little locking motion over her lips.

"Well…I guess I'm happy for you, Marcy. I need to see James for a moment."

"Of course. Go right ahead. I'm sure he wants to see you. He's just crazy about you, you know?"

Chloe nodded, not sure herself how much James might want to see her, but she felt like she had to see him.

She walked into his office and found him behind his desk, talking on the phone and scribbling down notes on a pad of paper in front of him. He looked…uneasy, she decided, was the best way to describe it, at seeing her. He held up a hand to signal that he'd just be a minute and offered her a chair.

Chloe took one of the big, comfy chairs across from his desk and a moment later, he put down the phone and came to lean against the other side of the desk in front of her. She wished he wasn't so close and that he didn't look so good at practically every moment of his life, even with a slightly blackened eye. She tried hard to wish that she'd never met him, but couldn't quite manage that.

"So," she began, "Marcy's going to work on a TV gossip show?"

James nodded.

"Do you think that's wise?"

"Not for the rest of the world, and I feel a little guilty about that. But she's happy, and she won't be messing with my life or yours anymore." He shrugged. "She had to go. I was afraid if I just fired her, she'd spill her guts about you and me on TV in a minute. I look at this as a major incentive for her to keep quiet."

"And…maybe as something that would make her happy?" Chloe suggested, because she thought deep down, he did like Marcy, crazy as she could be.

"People should do what they want, what they like. It tends to make us happy," he said, turning it all back around to him and her neatly and quickly. "What do you want, Chloe?"

And he didn't say it like, *Why are you here, Chloe?* He said it like, *What do you really want, Chloe?*

"Adam said you have a multimillion-dollar deal that's falling apart because your partner thinks you're mentally unstable. Because of me."

He shrugged easily, confidently. "Don't worry about it. I'll handle it."

"I can't help it. I feel really bad about that," she said.

Again, that easy, confident shrug, as if the whole thing meant nothing.

And she couldn't quite bring herself to say, *Adam said you didn't want to fake marry me at all, that you wanted something else. What did you really want?*

"I'm sorry about the money, Chloe," he said finally. "I didn't see another way to give you what you wanted—to be able to stay in business—without making that promise to Adam."

"You're saying that's why you did it? Just so I could stay in business?"

"Of course. Why else would I do it?"

"I don't know...."

"It wasn't some bid to keep me in your life or to still have some kind of control over you. I just wanted you to be happy. If you'd turned a profit, you and Adam would have been partners, and you never would have known about why he agreed to step in in the first place. Done deal."

"Really?"

"Of course. Did you really think I'd come back someday and use it as leverage to get you to...I don't know. Let me back into your life?"

She shrugged. It sounded silly when he said it like that. "It just seems odd that...I mean, we'd just broken up. I was so mad. It seemed like you were, too. Why would you care if my business went under or not for lack of an investor?"

"Because it was your dream. Because you'd worked so hard to get to where you were. Because I couldn't stand to be the one who took all that away from you, when it was only money. That amount didn't mean anything to me." He shrugged. "So why would I take it back, when it would mean taking everything away from you?"

Which sounded incredibly generous and kind of sweet.

She always ended up thinking he was really a nice person, when he wasn't making her mad. He just confused her so much. She had a hard time staying mad at him.

Money. They'd been talking about money.

"So, what are you going to do now about the money?" she asked.

He looked confused. "I wasn't planning on doing anything. What do you want me to do?"

"Nothing, I guess." Now she was even more confused.

"I promise I won't do anything else unless you specifically ask me to. That's what you want, right?"

"Yes," she said. "The company is mine. If I mess it all up, run it into the ground, kill it with my love life, that's on me."

He nodded. "Okay. We'll let things play out. If you turn things around, turn a profit, you and Adam will be partners in whatever happens in the future, and if not…I guess we'll figure out how to handle things then."

"I'll owe you a ton of money," she said.

He shrugged, as if it was nothing. "Whatever you want."

"Promise," she demanded.

"I promise."

"Good."

She sat there and waited. He gave the impression of a man who was a model of patience, which she knew was far from true. Which made her nervous. She still thought he was up to something.

"I'm…sorry I yelled at you yesterday."

He looked puzzled. "When?"

"When I told you…you know…that I was done. No more pretend…anything."

He shook his head. "Chloe, I'm good with that."

"You are?" Because he'd seemed really mad at the time. Of course, she had been, too.

"I don't want to pretend anymore about anything," he said.

That was too easy. She blinked up at him. "What do you mean?"

"I mean, I thought we had started something real. There was the fake stuff we were trying to save your business, and then, there was us, again, together, because it was what we wanted. Isn't that what we were doing?"

"I… Well…I thought so," she admitted.

"How did all that get lost in the middle of things yesterday? You, me, what's real?"

"I don't know. You were so mad at me," she began.

"You ran out on me? One minute, we're in my bed again, finally, and you finally let me tell you how sorry I am about the way things ended between us in the first place and about Giselle. Then I wake up, and you're gone?"

"I'm sorry," she said.

"You drugged me to get me to sleep so you could run out on me?"

"I didn't drug you so I could run away. I brought you those pills because the doctor said you were supposed to take them, and you were obviously uncomfortable and having trouble sleeping," she said, defending herself.

"Well, it so happens I didn't want to sleep. I wanted

that night with you. I'd waited damned long enough for it. I wasn't about to miss it."

She took a breath. "You were hurt."

"It wasn't like I was dying." He got this awful look on his face. "I thought you were happy. I thought that night meant something to you. And then I woke up, and you'd run away."

"I…I didn't know how I felt about…what happened."

"Well, I get that, Chloe. I do. Just tell me that. But don't run away. Not from me. Not again. Please?"

That was kind of sweet, Chloe admitted to herself, at least until she thought about the things he'd said the next morning.

"Wait a minute, you were the one spouting off all the fake stuff. You wanted a fake engagement, a fake marriage. That wasn't me. That was you."

"Yeah. I guess I might have panicked a little myself that morning," he admitted.

She gaped at him. He'd admitted to an emotion like panic?

"You drugged me," he reminded her. "Ran out on me, and then I found you kissing another man—"

"He was kissing me. I was too shocked to stop him. That's all."

"Okay, he was kissing you."

"Why would you be in a panic over Bryce grabbing me and kissing me?"

"I wasn't. I was just plain mad about that, and then you said you were giving up. If we weren't pretending to be a couple to save your business, I was afraid you might not see me at all. That's when I panicked." He shrugged, looking not arrogant at all. Looking astonishingly gorgeous and oddly human at the same time.

"Oh," Chloe said, her heart melting dangerously.

She was so far from being over him.

"I was just looking for a reason for you to have to see me, even if it was a fake reason," he said, grinning at her.

She fought the urge to throw herself in his arms, at least for the moment. She could worry about all their issues later. After she kissed him silly. She was thinking about doing just that, and from the look on his face, she thought maybe he was doing the same thing.

"So, what are you doing tomorrow night?" he asked finally.

"I'm not sure. Why?"

"Because people seem to think I'm despondent over losing you, and one of those people is a partner in a business deal I've been working on for six months. He's getting an award tomorrow night from the mayor for all the charity work he does."

"You're trying to hold your business deal together?" she asked. "How are you going to do that?"

"The easiest way would seem to be showing my business partner I am neither suicidal, nor have I lost you."

"But, we said no more games, no more lies—"

He stood up, pulled her to her feet, cupped the side of her face in his palm and asked, "Have I lost you, Chloe?"

"No," she whispered.

"Well, there you go." He backed up, let his hand drop to his side, and she could breathe again.

"It just seems like the same thing we've been doing," she said, when she could think again.

"I've got a lot of time and money invested in this deal already. I really want to save it, so I'm going to this dinner," he explained.

"Of course. I understand that."

"And I'd like to have you by my side, because I like it when you're with me. I want to see you. I want to dance with you. I want to try to convince you to come home with me afterward and hope you don't run away this time. That's what I want. What do you want, Chloe?"

Well, when he put it like that, it was really quite simple. They were doing what they wanted, what was real.

"I like it when I'm with you, too," she said. "I'll go."

"I don't understand," Addie said that afternoon, as they looked through a rack of dresses in the shop to find one Connie could alter for Chloe to use as a formal gown. "I thought you said you two were giving up. No more games."

"We're not playing games. We're going to the mayor's charity awards dinner," Chloe insisted.

"But, how is that not pretending?"

"We're just not. No fake stories leaked to the press. No tipping off photographers. No fake strategies to try to make me look as if I'm not cursed."

"But, how is that really different from before?"

Chloe was a bit perplexed herself. "When he explained it, it sounded perfectly reasonable."

"Of course."

"No, really," Chloe insisted. "I want to see him. He wants to see me. So we're going out together."

"To the same sort of event we would have picked if we were still playing the save-the-business game that's proven to be so disastrous for us all. Do I need to remind you of any of this?"

"No. But I still want to be there with him. Besides, I'd hate it if all this started messing with his business, too. I feel guilty enough about my business going under. I'm not going to let his be hurt, too," she said.

"Nothing is going to damage his business," Addie argued. "The man has a fortune. He'll always have a fortune. If it's not quite as big as it used to be, he'll get by just fine."

"I want to be the woman who's standing by his side helping him fix this. It's no great challenge to gaze up at him adoringly in the middle of a fancy party, and it's not any kind of a lie. I always want to be with him, Addie. I've wanted that ever since we broke up in the first place. I was just too mad and too hurt to do anything about it."

Addie groaned and buried her face in her hands. "Please, please, please don't say that—"

"Whether I say it or not, it's still true. I want to be with him."

"He will break your heart again—"

"Or maybe he won't. Maybe he'll take really good care of my heart this time. Maybe we'll be better with each other, better to each other. Maybe we learned something from the last time and the time we spent apart. I mean, people are capable of changing. I need to believe that for myself, that I can grow and learn and change."

Addie just stared, looking like Chloe had announced she had a terminal disease or something.

"And if none of that's true, and I really am cursed in love," Chloe said, "I want to be cursed in love with him."

Still, nothing from Addie.

"Please say something," Chloe begged.

"If he hurts you again…"

"I know," Chloe said.

And then she found the dress she'd been looking for, a heavy milky-white silk gown, deceptively simple in front, save for the heavy line of shimmery silver beading at the neckline, plunging into a daringly low dip in back, again simple as could be but lined in silver beading.

It was for a woman who loved her back and hips.

Chloe was okay with her back, but she couldn't say she

was all that crazy about her hips. James, however, was. If she could make it easier for him to gaze at her adoringly, she was doing her part.

"Do you want his hands all over you?" Addie asked when she saw the back of the dress. "Because this is a dress for a woman who wants a man's hands all over her."

"I want to look like a woman who would dazzle him," she said. "And I wouldn't mind tormenting him a bit. We'll be surrounded by people. The mayor will be there. What's going to happen at a charity ball?"

Addie shook her head. "If that's what you really want, let's go try this on you and see what kind of alterations Connie can do."

They were headed for one of the big dressing rooms, when Robbie stopped them, pointing out a deliveryman with what looked like an old-fashioned trunk.

"It's from him," Robbie said. He was avoiding saying James's name unless he absolutely had to.

"Oh, now he's going to start with fancy presents?" Addie was definitely skeptical about that.

Chloe wasn't sure how she felt about it. He'd tried that the first time, showering her with expensive things, until she'd put her foot down and made him stop. It just seemed too easy for him, too smooth, too practiced a thing, and one that didn't really mean anything at all. She suspected his assistant picked out most of the presents he'd sent.

This looked…different. Very different.

"It's from Italy," Robbie said, signing for it. "I feel like I should recognize the name of the town for some reason."

He gave the pronunciation his best shot.

Chloe gasped. "Lace. The area's famous for its gorgeous handmade lace."

They finally got the trunk open. It was, truly, an ancient steamer trunk, and there, packed carefully in thin tissue paper, was lace so delicate and beautiful Chloe almost cried.

Lace was the most expensive part of wedding gowns, the most intricate, elaborate, fanciful part. She indulged when she could, but this was a veritable treasure chest of various handmade laces from an area of Italy known for producing some of the best in the world.

It was like giving a painter the finest set of paints, like giving a child the most delightful and thoughtful present ever. Terribly extravagant, and yet, the perfect gift for someone in Chloe's profession.

Robbie whistled. "I have to admit, the man's stepping up his game."

Yes, he was.

Chloe took the lace out piece by piece, studying each one, exclaiming over the delicacy, the workmanship, the things she'd like to do with each one. And she was utterly charmed and touched by what he'd done.

James stayed away for the three days until the party. It just about killed him, but he did it. He feared if he pushed too hard too soon, she would only retreat further, and he didn't want that to happen.

He sent presents instead. The lace, which he'd heard was a big hit. A special blend of gourmet coffee that he drank, because while she called him a coffee snob, she always raved about the coffee he kept at his apartment. And today he picked out diamond earrings to go with the gown Addie said Chloe planned to wear tonight.

He got to the house a little early, because he still had some bruises from the accident, and Addie insisted he allow one of their makeup artists to try to cover them. When he objected, she said, "Do you want to go to this party looking like a man who took a walk in traffic four days ago?"

No, he did not, so he arrived early and let them do what they wanted to him. He had to admit when it was done, he could hardly tell he'd been in an accident.

Then he spotted Chloe halfway down the fancy, old-fashioned, curving staircase in a simple, glossy dress in a shade that made him think of milk. It was all but sleeveless, with a wide but delicate band of sparkling silver beads and things following the simple V neckline. Connie came down the stairs behind Chloe and draped a matching cape over her shoulder that fastened with a little silver chain in front.

Addie had been right to suggest he get earrings, he saw now. A necklace would have been all wrong with this gown.

James took a breath and walked over to the bottom of the staircase to meet Chloe, who had her hair piled on top of her head in one of those effortless-looking knots she wore so often, which showed off her neck and shoulders to perfection. She looked a little nervous, a little uneasy as she caught her breath and smiled up at him.

"You're like a medieval snow princess," he said, catching her lightly by the arms and leaning down, intending to kiss her softly.

"No, no, no. You don't touch so much as a hair on her head until after you get past the photographers on your way inside the party," Addie told him. "You two may not care anymore, but I do. Promise me?"

He promised. He could wait. But barely.

He pulled the little jewelry box out of the pocket of his tuxedo jacket instead and held it out to Chloe.

She frowned. "We're going to have to talk about this, James."

"Okay, but for now, these, I'm told, will look perfect with your dress." When she shot him a questioning look, he said, "I had help."

Addie had sent a photo to his phone that showed the glossy white of the dress and a bit of that silver trim, which he'd shown to the clerk at the jewelry store, who'd then pulled out a number of earrings she said would be appropriate.

Chloe took the box and opened it up, staring down at what he'd thought was a very plain line of diamonds to hang from each earlobe. But having seen the dress, he understood. Anything more would have been too much.

Chloe looked inordinately pleased with them, and he stood there while she put them on, then let Addie, Connie and Robbie look her over.

Addie gave her a handful of sparkly silver bracelets that went on both arms. Connie handed her a very tiny, silver bejeweled purse, and Robbie fooled with the cape until he was completely happy with the way it draped. They finally proclaimed her perfect and turned her over to him.

He tried to be a model of good behavior and courtesy, helping her out the door and into the limousine. Then he settled in on the far side of the big backseat and simply stared at her.

"You look like you want to nibble on me," she said finally, staring back at him.

"I do. I want to do a lot more than that, but I promised not to muss you up. You stay over there, and I'll stay over here, and we just might make it. But you should know now, there won't be any room between us on the way home after the party."

She seemed as if she wanted to make it harder for him to keep his distance now, and he got the feeling that she was up to something. She and her coconspirators back at the showroom.

But she didn't do anything, just sat there looking regal, like a woman from another era. He was already thinking about just how long they had to stay at the party. She was coming home with him tonight—another thing he'd already decided—and she would not be sneaking out the next morning.

By the time they finally pulled up to the party, he was in really bad shape, having mentally undressed her at least a dozen times. He was doubting his own ability not to ravish her in the nearest small, dark, enclosed space he could find.

He stepped out of the limousine and into the lights. One of tonight's award recipients was a well-known Broadway star, and the mayor was toying with a run for president, so Addie had predicted an abundance of media coverage. She was right.

In their time in the spotlight, James had discovered that if he kept his attention on Chloe, he didn't mind the cameras so much. He smiled with genuine pleasure and pride as he reached into the limousine to help Chloe out. He was more than happy to show her off. He wanted the world to know she was his.

The gown's glossy fabric with its silver embellishments came alive under the lights, and she positively glowed as they posed together for the cameras for a long moment. Then she undid the catch on her cape and peeled that off. He leaned in to her side for one more picture, put a hand to the small of her back, where it had been moments before, and found...

Nothing but bare skin beneath his palm.

He sucked in a breath.

She shot him another one of those little secret, mischievous looks that again told him she was definitely up to something.

"Chloe," he said, feeling like he was choking. "Did you forget something?"

"I don't think so." She blinked up at him innocently.

"There's no back to your dress."

"Of course there is."

He let his hand ease lower and lower still—to skin and more skin. He found himself nearly cupping her bottom before he finally hit dress. And then he didn't know what to do.

She obviously wasn't naked. But he didn't think he could stand beside her all night—or even worse, have her in his arms, dancing—in this dress, with all this luscious skin to see and touch. He didn't think he could speak.

Chloe laughed softly, the sound reverberating through his body, and then turned around, one of her palms pressed flat against his chest, smiling over her shoulder as she showed off the back of the gown to the cameras.

There were a few appreciative whistles from the almost exclusively male photographers, and then they started talking to her, encouraging her to look this way and that, telling her how beautiful she was tonight.

He told himself not to look, knew it was the smart thing to do. His best shot was to stand there like a mute statue.

But then she turned back around. She was a step ahead of him now, and all he did was look down, and there it was, her entire back bared for him to see, framed with that wide band of delicate silver embellishment that ended in a V just a hint above her hips.

He saw that pretty curve of her neck, the delicate bones of her shoulders, the subtle outline of her spine, but the thing that was killing him—just absolutely killing him— was the way the dress followed the indention at the base of her spine and then flared out, cupping that perfect bottom of hers.

His first thought, when he was capable of thinking, was to wonder exactly how much or how little she was wearing under that dress. His second—even more unsettling—was that it seemed with no effort at all, he could slide a hand down the back of the dress and onto her bare bottom. He really thought she might be completely bare under the gown.

"Do you like it?" she whispered without looking at him, without interfering with the view he had of all that delicious skin of hers.

He grunted, words failing him.

She laughed softly, and he didn't care about the cameras or anyone else anymore. He pulled her into his arms for a quick, deep kiss.

Chapter Twelve

Chloe thought the evening went as well as it possibly could, all things considered. They posed for photos, looking, she hoped, like a normal, happy couple, no one suicidal, no one cheating, no one cursed in love.

Inside, people at the event stared, most smiled politely, many whispered furiously among themselves as Chloe and James walked past them. Chloe didn't like it, but it wasn't as bad as she feared, either. No one said anything outrageously catty to her face. The other women kept their distance for the most part, and even when they didn't, James kept Chloe plastered to his side. No one got closer than she did, which she found highly pleasing.

And her gown seemed to be a big hit, judging by the things she heard from the photographers outside and as she and James walked through the room. She was always happy when people were admiring one of her gowns.

But not even people's reaction to her design could hold her attention.

That was all on James.

He was practically eating her up with his eyes. He hadn't taken them off of her, and he'd hardly said a word to anyone else as they drank champagne, nibbled on appetizers, nodded to a few acquaintances.

Then he got her on the dance floor, in his arms, and kept her there. He was so smooth, so elegant, holding her so that their bodies were brushing against each other, just barely, just enough to drive her crazy. She tried to get closer, but he wouldn't let her. And having his hand on the bare skin at the small of her back, in public, was starting to get to her, to feel a little wicked and forbidden, in the same way she imagined he'd felt when he'd first discovered the way the dress was made.

He kept it up, advancing and retreating, looking down at her with that heated gaze of his, and yet looking so cool and controlled, and she started to get it.

"This is payback for the dress?" she whispered to him.

He leaned down and took a little nibble on her earlobe, sending a shiver all the way down to her toes. "This is just the beginning of payback for the dress."

She laughed. No sense in lying to herself. This was what she wanted when she'd chosen this dress. To be irresistible to him and to end up back in his bed. She wasn't going to fight it any longer. They were doing what they wanted now, and she wanted him.

His hand slid lower on her back, just below the edge of the fabric at her hip, just for a moment. She arched her back and pressed her lower body to his, felt the unmistakable pressure of his aroused body and sucked in a breath.

In the end, they didn't stay as long as she expected at the party. She wasn't even sure they'd talked to the man he'd come here to see. It was all a blur of his heated gaze and possessive touch and anticipation of what was to come.

He got her into the back of the limousine, in the privacy there in the dark, him in the far corner and her leaning into him, as he slid that hand down her back once more. This time the hand didn't stop, easing below the dress and pausing briefly over the wide swath of lace of her panties, then slipping inside those, too, landing in a sexy, heated possessiveness on her bare bottom.

He swore softly and at length, savoring the touch. She dared to laugh, and he silenced her with his mouth on hers. He kept his hand where it was and kept right on kissing her until the limousine stopped and they had to get out.

She saw that they were at his apartment building.

He led her inside the building, into his apartment, into his bedroom, turned her to face the wall and then leaned into her with that big, powerful, unmistakably aroused body of his and started nuzzling her neck like a man who had all night to do it.

Payback time for tormenting him with the backless dress.

Chloe was glad she had the wall for support as he fought his own impatience and hers and took his time working slowly over her neck with his lips, his tongue, his teeth, his hands on either side of her bottom, his body firmly settled into the notch of her hips.

It was an all-out assault as he slowly worked his way down her back, ending up on his knees, his mouth finally settling into that incredibly sensitive spot at the base of her spine.

She could barely stand by then, her legs turned to jelly, her whole body trembling, only the weight of his body pressed against hers keeping her upright.

His hands slid back up to her breasts, cupping them,

teasing at her nipples, one hand slipping between her legs. And there was something about that spot on her back and his mouth there, sending all those delicious sensations up her entire spine, that made it feel like his mouth was everywhere, all over her body at once.

He would not stop, kept going until she literally screamed with the pleasure shooting through her body.

And then, looking very, very satisfied with himself, he turned her around, stripped her bare, lowered her onto her back on his bed and then stood in front of her, methodically stripping off his own clothes piece by piece. She lay there naked on the bed, eating him up with her eyes and having to wait until he was done undressing himself to touch him.

Then he climbed onto the bed on top of her and slid that deliciously, hotly aroused body of his inside of hers, inch by wondrous inch. She whimpered. She begged, but nothing worked. He hardly even breathed, it seemed, until he was damned good and ready, pushing her effortlessly, beautifully up over the edge and into oblivion.

She slept blissfully, snuggling with him, opening her arms to him deep in the night and welcoming him back into her body for more, waking the next morning naked in that big bed of his.

Chloe rolled over and found him awake and watching her, his perfect hair just a little mussed up, a sexy shadow of stubble on his face, looking at her with a gaze that was both possessive and very, very satisfied.

He leaned over and brushed her hair back from her face, then kissed her cheek. "Good morning."

"Good morning."

"No regrets this morning?" he asked.

"No regrets. And I didn't run away, either."

"You wouldn't have gotten far. I had the place booby-trapped after the last time. You would have set off all kinds of alarms, which would have woken me up, and I would have stopped you."

"Booby-trapped?"

He grinned wickedly. "It was that or handcuff you to the bed, which offered certain advantages of its own. Maybe next time...."

Chloe put a hand on that stubbly jaw of his, thinking about how much she loved seeing him a little mussed up, because it was such a rare thing with him, always so cool and controlled, so polished, so self-assured.

She leaned in to kiss him, thinking to pull him down on top of her, not ready for their magical night to end.

The next time she woke up, he wasn't in the bed beside her, but she smelled his favorite coffee brewing and a moment later, he walked out of the bathroom, steam billowing out behind him along with a delicious, manly scent she always associated with him. His hair was wet, and he was wearing nothing but a formfitting pair of workout pants riding low on his hips.

She leaned back against the pillows and grinned at him, and he grinned back.

"Coffee?" he asked.

"Yes, please."

He was back a moment later with a steaming cup for her and one for himself. Chloe sat up in the bed, the sheet wrapped around her chest, her hair going every which way. He sat on the side of the bed, facing her.

"Could you just stay here in my bedroom for a week or so, just you and me, nobody else? We have coffee, and we can have food delivered. We won't starve."

"You would never stay away from your office for a

week. They'd think you died and send someone to investigate."

"I'd call in, tell them I'm okay—"

"They'd never believe it. Besides, you have a big business deal and I have a company to save."

"I don't want to let you leave," he confessed, leaning forward to kiss her softly.

"Believe me, I don't want to go. But I have to make a lot of money, so I can keep my company afloat and so you and I are never partners in business again."

"You don't have to do that, Chloe."

"Yes, I do. I should never have let you invest in my business in the first place. It was too much. Everything went downhill from there for us."

"I wanted to do it. I wanted you to have what you'd always dreamed of, what you'd worked so hard for."

She gave him another quick kiss. "I know you did, but it just got to where it all scared me so much. I was in love with you, and that already gave you so much power over me. To have the other big thing in my life—my work—dependent on you, too… It meant my whole life was wrapped up in you, and given the fact that I'd never had a relationship with a man that had really worked…I couldn't handle it. I felt like you had way too much control over me," she admitted.

He shook his head. "And I always felt like I had next to none with you. That you were a woman who does exactly as she pleases, and no man could ever keep you from doing that. It left me feeling a little vulnerable, powerless, even, which was not something I was accustomed to."

James? Vulnerable? It wasn't a word she would have ever associated with him.

"So, we were both scared of the power we had over each

other. I never would have guessed that. I felt so inept as a businesswoman next to you."

"Well." He shrugged, smiled. "I wouldn't want you to be my accountant or make my business plan, but there are plenty of people with those skills. You, Chloe…you're brilliant. You have an amazing creative mind. I always admired that so much."

She sucked in a breath. Brilliant? "Really?"

"Yes. I fell so hard for you that first night we met, at your fashion show, watching you work. All the energy you had, the intensity you brought to getting everything just right, the joy in seeing what you'd created. You are like no other woman I've ever known. Did I not show you that? Make you feel like that?"

She pushed her hair back behind her ear and looked away, tearing up a little bit. "I don't know. I think, mostly, you just made me feel so much of everything. It was so intense, so overwhelming. I got scared. I started looking for things that were wrong or sure to go wrong. I've been thinking a lot about the last few days we were together, and I know I was pushing you away—"

"Tell me you believe me about what happened with Giselle," he said, taking her chin in his hand and turning her face to his, his gaze locked on hers. "I am so sorry, Chloe. So sorry I hurt you that way. I will always regret it."

"I believe we were lousy at trusting each other, and I pushed you away, and if you hadn't done something like that with her to blow up our relationship, I would have blown it up myself before long. I've done it before."

"You believe me?" he asked again.

"I do."

All the breath went out of him. He dipped his head down low, and when he raised it again, his eyes were glistening with moisture. "I wasn't sure I'd ever hear you say that."

He kissed her softly, took his thumb and brushed a tear from her cheek.

"I love you, Chloe. I'll never stop."

Chloe felt like her heart flipped over in her chest.

James laughed just a bit. "You look like you were afraid I was going to say that."

"A little afraid," she admitted. "But happy, too. Very happy. I want this to work. I want that so much. I was miserable without you."

"Me, too," he admitted. "And that's enough for now. I won't push. The next time I propose, you'd better not laugh at me."

"You didn't propose!"

"I said, 'Marry me.' And you laughed. I remember. I was there."

"You weren't serious!"

"I was—"

"Two seconds later, you said, 'Fake marry me.' And that made me so mad!"

"Okay, I didn't handle it well. I freely admit that. But I didn't go to the fake thing until you laughed at the real thing, and I told you, I only did that because I thought you might not see me again if we gave up on the plan to save your business."

"You don't have to marry me to see me again," she offered.

He looked ridiculously pleased with himself, despite the whole fake-marry-me thing. "Good. And you don't have to answer me right now about marrying me for real. I just said it because…I wanted to say it. I want you to know how I feel, but not to freak you out. Please tell me I didn't freak you out too badly."

"I…I'm still here. I didn't run away."

"Okay, I'll accept that."

"James, I have to fix this mess with my business. It's just something I have to do."

"Okay. I want you to be happy, Chloe. I want you to have absolutely everything you want in life. And I want you to know, whatever it takes to get your business through this crisis, money-wise, it's yours. I won't let you go under."

"No, you can't do that. I have to do it myself. I can't be this pitiful, inept woman you bail out of trouble, every time something goes wrong with her company. You have to stay out of it."

He made a face. "I don't think you're a pitiful or inept woman. I just love you, and to me, that means I'm never going to stand by and do nothing when you're in trouble. I am always going to try to fix things for you. How is this a bad thing?"

She took his face in her hands. "That's sweet. It's very sweet, and if that's why you came to my rescue when the whole runway-brawl thing came out—"

"That and because I was dying to see you again."

"Thank you. Really. I mean it. I've never had a man I felt like I could count on to have my back that way, and it means a lot to me," she said sincerely. "But I still have to do this myself. And you have to let me. No matter how hard that is for you. My business can't exist just because I have a rich boyfriend who'll keep writing checks to let us stay in business. It's too important to me and to who I am."

"I never saw it as anything like a hobby, I swear."

"No more sneaking around behind my back to fix things."

"Okay."

"Promise me. We don't want to be the same two people, making the same mistakes all over again. Remember?"

"I promise."

James had his regular driver take Chloe home, and she sat in the backseat of the town car in her dress and her cape, feeling like Cinderella whose ball had simply never ended.

She made it home before the shop opened that morning, even managed to get to her room, shower and dress before anyone found her. She got back downstairs, got some of the great coffee made from the stash that James had sent over.

She walked into the showroom, finding Addie sitting on the platform viewing area in front of the big mirrors drinking her coffee, as well. Chloe sat down beside her, and Addie tossed a tabloid on the floor in front of them, with a picture of Chloe and James on the cover.

"Wow, the dress looks great," Chloe said.

"Yes, it does. And you have that sickening little glow about you that... Well, I have to admit, it works in the shot." Then she added another tabloid on the pile. "James looks like he might need someone to perform the Heimlich maneuver on him in this one. Not that it's a bad look on him. I don't think the man could take a bad picture."

"I think he'd just gotten a look at the back of my dress. He liked it," Chloe said, thinking about when he'd kissed his way down her back.

"Okay, don't go all gooey on me. I'm not up to that," Addie protested. "I'm just saying...last night worked for us. Not that it was your aim. I understand that. Really, I do. I just...don't know what's going to happen. We've stopped the company's nosedive, at least. Which is big. Of course, God only knows what might happen tomorrow, with our luck, and we have so little available cash, even with the last check Adam wrote us."

"Yeah, about that…" Chloe began, telling Addie it really hadn't been Adam. It had been James all along.

"And you're okay with that?" Addie asked when Chloe had gotten the whole story out. "With a man as secretive, as manipulative and as controlling as that?"

"He said he did it because he loves me, and he couldn't stand by and do nothing while I was about to lose something he knows I love."

Addie made a face and groaned.

"It was sweet, really, the way he explained it," Chloe protested.

"And you believed him?"

"Yes, I did. You make him out to be some kind of monster, Addie, and maybe that's partly my fault, because I was so mad and so hurt when we broke up the first time. But he's not a monster. He's someone who's not all that good at relationships or trusting people, and neither am I."

"That's what you think?"

"Yes, I think we were two scared, screwed up people in love, making a mess of things and hurting each other. I know I hurt him, too. I really did. And I know I did things I regret. But I'm still crazy about him, and I want this chance with him. That means forgiving and forgetting."

"Oh, that's convenient—"

"If it's about the money and Adam… If he hadn't made Adam those promises, Adam wouldn't be here. We'd either still have been partners with James all along or we'd have been out of business a year and a half ago. Did you think about that?"

Addie fumed silently for a moment, then said, "He lied to you about it."

"Okay, yes, but it wasn't malicious, and I don't see how

it was any kind of effort at controlling me. It kept us in business, and we never heard from him, not until a few weeks ago when all hell broke loose. You can't believe he had some evil plan to force himself back into my life and waited a year and a half to spring it."

That got Addie thinking at least. "I didn't see it that way," she finally admitted. "I'm afraid he really wants to marry you this time. What are you going to say when he asks?"

Chloe wasn't quite ready to own up to the fact that he already had. That was her own sweet, little secret for now. She wasn't even sure how she felt about it yet. "That there's something really pathetic about a woman getting engaged for the fourth time. I already told him I was never getting engaged again."

"Okay, but one does not have to be engaged to be married," Addie pointed out.

"I know that." Chloe sighed.

"Well, the upside is, this whole non-fake romance of yours is a big hit. You are no longer cursed in love, and we are actually limping along fairly well right now. Limping, but going in the right direction, business-wise. I think we may just survive this, and maybe, one day, even pay off your boyfriend for his sneaky, underhanded investment in the company."

"Why is it working now?" Chloe asked.

"Because you're not pretending anymore. You and James are crazy about each other, and it shows in every photo anyone's snapped of you."

"I am absolutely crazy about him," she admitted. "And I'm not as scared as I used to be."

"Well, that's progress," Addie admitted.

"Oh, did I tell you Marcy's gone? James got a friend

of a friend to give her a job as an assistant at a reality TV show. She's so much happier now."

"Wonder what that cost him?"

"He wouldn't say, just that it was worth every cent."

Addie laughed. "He really paid to get rid of her?"

"I think the producer's wife heads a children's charity, and he just gave them a really nice donation, and Marcy got a job. It worked." Chloe shrugged. "He really is a wonderful man."

"You should probably know that I'm prepared to tolerate him. For your sake," Addie said.

Chloe hugged her. With Addie, that was progress!

Now she just had to figure out what to do with the man.

Chapter Thirteen

They had a good week. An incredibly normal, very good week. James took her to the opening of a Broadway play, to a gallery opening where he wanted help picking out some artwork as an investment and for the bare walls of his apartment, and to a benefit for a children's hospital.

Brides stopped freaking out. They even had some walk-in traffic, women not ordering dresses, but trying them on and probably trying to figure out if things were truly stabilizing at the design house.

They were no longer a constant presence on tabloid covers or the subject of ludicrous rumors on blogs. It seemed a relationship going well was simply not tabloid fodder.

Tonight James was taking Chloe to a fancy cocktail party hosted by the investor who'd been so nervous about doing business with James a couple weeks before.

Chloe had taken apart one of her gowns, floor-length with a sheer over layer in pale gold tulle, heavily embel-

lished with burnt-gold leaf and beading, which had looked
elegant and very bridal over a long, cream-colored silk
sheath. Instead she put it over a clingy, stretchy, fitted
minidress, which turned the whole outfit into something
sexy, elegant and unusual.

She loved the way James's eyes got that slightly dazed
look, coupled with a blast of sheer heat, when he looked
at her in it.

He would hardly touch her in the car on the way to the
party. It had gotten to be a habit, his trying so hard to keep
his hands off her on the way to an event, flirting outrageously with her while there. He'd be all over her in the car
on the way back to his apartment, and they'd barely make
it inside before he stripped her bare and had his wicked
way with her. As foreplay went, it worked really well for
Chloe.

He was such a beautiful man, so perfectly put together,
so elegant, so controlled, which made it so much more
thrilling to see how hard he had to fight for that control
when it came to her and how satisfying it was when he
lost it.

The evening was running entirely true to form. Little
innocent touches here, a polite hand there, long, steamy,
appreciative looks and wicked, whispered promises of
things to come. Chloe suspected they would be leaving
indecently early once again.

"Five minutes," James whispered to her. "I just have to
talk to one more person, and then we're out of here."

Chloe nodded, nibbled on a cream tart and then saw
a redheaded woman in a dress that was absolutely to die
for. She sometimes stalked women in really great dresses
to get a nice, long look at the designs, and ended up in a
quiet hallway, spying on the woman in another room. The

dress was asymmetrical, a design technique Chloe seldom got to play with.

As she stepped to the right, to maintain her view of the great dress, she bumped into one of the servers working the party.

"I'm so sorry," she began, then realized he looked familiar.

He did a double take when he saw her, surprised, highly appreciative and a little embarrassed. "Chloe! It's you! You look…amazing and all grown up."

Chloe just nodded. "Charlie, I can't believe you're here."

This was Fiancé No. 1, the boy she'd supposedly walked out on because she wanted her career more than she wanted him. Which wasn't exactly true. For a time, she'd wanted both. But Charlie hadn't wanted her to want anyone or anything but him. She felt the slightest flicker of unease, because this was really strange, having him showing up here now.

"I am so happy you're here," he said, handing his tray off to a passing server, and steering her down the hallway where it was quieter. "I actually wondered if you might be. It sounded like the fancy kind of party you might go to. I've been thinking about you a lot lately. Seeing your picture all over the place."

Chloe nodded. "It's been an interesting month."

"Miss me? Just a little?"

She smiled, wanting to be polite and friendly, at least. "Sure, I do."

He got a huge grin on his face. "I've missed you like crazy, Chloe. The time when we were together was the best time of my life."

He grabbed her by the arms and held on to her, smiling down at her with that goofy smile she'd loved in high school, when they'd first gotten together, and those sad puppy-dog eyes of his made her feel like she was sixteen again, at least for a moment. And then, before she realized what was going on, he pulled her close and started kissing her.

Chloe stood there, shocked into a kind of paralysis at first, and then finally came to her senses and pushed hard enough against his chest to get her mouth free of his. "What are you doing?"

"I think I might still love you, Chloe," he said, still hanging on to her. "I want us to have another chance."

She gaped at him. "Charlie…"

And then James was there, by her side, with a tight grip on her arm, pulling her away, and he looked absolutely furious. "James?"

"Are you two done?" he asked.

"Done?" she repeated.

"Yes, done."

"Yes, we're done," she said. "What is the matter with you?"

He shot her a murderous look and took off down the hall, dragging her along with him. He went through a door, turned down another hall and then pulled her inside a darkened room and shut the door behind them.

Then he started pacing, like he had too much energy shooting through his body for him to be still.

"What in the world was that?" she asked.

He glared at her. "Is this payback for what I did to you? Is it punishment?"

"No," she insisted.

"Because that's the second time I've walked in and found you kissing another man, and it's really starting to make me mad. And it makes me think maybe this is all a game to you. Maybe you never intended to give me another chance. Maybe you just wanted to pay me back for the way I hurt you a year and a half ago, and you know just how to do it. Just like that. Exactly what I saw in there."

Chloe was shocked that he could think that, that he could feel that way.

"James," she said, going to him, taking his face in her hands, to make him look at her. He looked devastated. "That was…he's a guy I haven't seen in five years. I had no idea he was going to do that. One minute we're talking about high school, and the next thing I know, he's kissing me. I was too stunned to even do anything for a moment. That's all."

"That's what you said about the other guy," he reminded her.

"The other guy was Bryce. You saw the video of the runway brawl, didn't you?"

He nodded tightly.

"Well, if I told you that guy would ever show up in my life again and want me back, wouldn't you be shocked, too? Would you ever think he'd have the nerve to say he wanted me back and grab me and try to kiss me?"

He didn't say a word.

"Oh, come on. Nobody could have seen that one coming. Even my life isn't normally as weird as that."

"And this guy?" he asked finally, calming down a little.

"I spent maybe two minutes with him. You probably saw the whole thing. We…we dated in high school. We were engaged right afterward."

"That's your first fiancé? Chloe, what do you do to us, that we just can't forget you? How many more of these guys are going to show up, wanting you back?"

"I don't—there aren't any more. Just the three of you. You're the only one left."

She kissed him softly on his mouth, thinking to soothe him, and he responded by hauling her against him and holding her so tight she could barely breathe. Tension radiated from him, and he was sucking in air like a man desperate for it.

When he finally let her go, she said, "James, you can't seriously think I'm playing some kind of game with you, can you?"

He still looked grim.

"You do? You're seriously jealous of me and a guy I haven't seen in years?"

"Hell, yes, I'm jealous!"

She'd hurt him. Really hurt him. And scared him. Which wasn't something she could do unless the feelings he had for her were every bit as big and strong and scary as the way she felt about him.

She hadn't really believed that until now.

James Elliott was crazy about her.

How about that?

"I'm sorry," she said. "I would never set out to deliberately hurt you. I couldn't." She took a breath, then admitted, "I am trying very hard not to let myself love you again—"

"I know you are. I absolutely know it. Hell, I'd have to be a fool not see it."

And he hated it. She could see that now, too.

He just stood there, a beautiful man in a perfectly fit tuxedo, hands in his pockets, sucking in air and staring at her, and she felt terrible about the way she'd hurt him.

"Will you take me home, please?" she asked finally.

He looked surprised and not happy.

"Your home, I mean."

They got out of there and into the limousine, where he sat holding her hand, watching her, not saying anything. When they got to his apartment, he made himself a drink and stood in the living room, slowly sipping Scotch.

"I'm sorry," she said finally. "I would never set out deliberately to hurt you or to trick you. I care too much about you to ever do that to you."

"Okay," he said, seeming to want to take the measure of each word she said and turn it over and over in his mind until he knew exactly what he felt about them.

She took the drink from his hand and then slid into his arms, which caught her to him so tightly. He was trembling, she realized, and for the first time, she truly believed that he was every bit as vulnerable and unsure of himself in this relationship as she was.

In this, they were equal. Finally. All the risks of being in love, being that vulnerable to another human being, were theirs to share. The rewards, too.

She reached up and kissed him softly, a kiss he turned hungry and urgent. She finally eased back and said, "Until tonight, I don't think I believed that everything you feel for me is every bit as big and overwhelming and scary as what I've always felt for you."

He stared down at her. "How could you not know that?"

"James, you're the strongest, most self-assured man I've ever met—"

"Not where you're concerned!"

"Well, I guess I didn't really believe that until now."

"That's all I had to do? Go nuts over some other man kissing you? I did that with Fiancé No. 3 weeks ago, remember?"

"I don't know. I just thought you were mad then. We weren't…in the same place where we are now. We hadn't talked through everything or spent as much time together yet, and I…I guess there was still that awful knot of fear inside me about letting myself go completely. About not trying to hold back and protect any part of myself from you anymore."

"And now?" he said urgently.

"I give up. We can be scared together. I love you."

He finally smiled. "Say that last part again?"

"I love you. I don't think I ever really stopped, even though I tried so hard not to."

"And you'll marry me? Because I need that. I need to know that we're both in this to stay this time. I want rings. I want vows. I want a signed piece of paper, and anything else I can think of. The whole thing."

"I was thinking we could start slowly? Like…maybe getting a marriage license?" she asked. "Because I looked online, and the thing is, you can get one and you don't have to use it. I mean, you can, but you don't have to. They give you sixty days, and if you haven't gotten married then, you can just go back and get another license and have another sixty days. You can keep doing that as long as you want."

"You want to get a marriage license and not use it?"

"It's a step. A first," she explained.

"Okay—"

"A statement of intent. How about that?"

He laughed. "I like that better. A statement of our intentions."

"I just…can't be engaged again. You have to understand that."

"But you're willing to get a marriage license?"

She nodded.

"Okay," he agreed. "That's a step."

"And I don't want to take months and plan some big thing. We'll just…go do it one day when we're ready. I want to make my own dress, and I'll use some of the lace you gave me. It's so beautiful. I want Addie to be my maid of honor. I need Robbie and Connie. Adam should be there and anybody you want. And you. That's it. Can it just be like that?"

"Chloe, as long as we end up married, I'll be happy."

"And I have to get my business back on track. I have to. Although, things are looking so much better lately. Being seen around the city with you has done wonders for business. And it's been weeks since anyone's said I'm cursed in love."

He kissed her long enough to leave her breathless. "No one will ever have a reason to say that again. I promise."

Epilogue

Celebrities About Town
A Channel 5 Web Exclusive
by Marcy Ellen Wade

Designer Chloe Allen always manages to surprise, and her spring show was no exception.

Instead of a mess of jilted lovers in a runway free-for-all, this time fashion critics and buyers were treated to a surprise wedding of none other than Chloe Allen herself to one of New York's most eligible bachelors, financial whiz James Elliott IV.

The couple had repeatedly denied being engaged, even though they'd been seen all over the city together. Public records show they had purchased multiple marriage licenses over the past few months, and Chloe had even been photographed wearing a gorgeous cushion-cut diamond on the third finger of her left hand.

Chloe's collection was particularly exquisite at this

show, elegant, polished and yet highly romantic, perhaps influenced by her newfound faith in love and that fourth engagement being the one that finally took for her?

Her collection came down the runway to massive applause, and then as guests mixed and mingled at a reception afterward, they found themselves invited back to the runway for the simple, surprisingly intimate and touching ceremony.

There, where it seemed Chloe's career and her personal life were left in tatters, stood the happy couple, looking radiant and simply unable to take their eyes off each other.

Ms. Allen's half sister and a partner in her business, Addison Grey, served as maid of honor. Her cousin Robert Allen performed the ceremony, and another cousin Constance Allen sang as the newlyweds had their first dance.

Rumor has it the couple first met when Chloe mistook James for a missing male model at one of her earlier fashion shows and tried to send him down the runway with a model wearing one of her wedding gowns.

Who would ever believe such a mistake would lead to a runway wedding of their own someday?

* * * * *

**Harlequin**®

COMING NEXT MONTH

Available September 27, 2011

SPECIAL EDITION™

REQUEST YOUR FREE BOOKS!
2 FREE NOVELS PLUS 2 FREE GIFTS!

◆ Harlequin®

SPECIAL EDITION
Life, Love & Family

YES! Please send me 2 FREE Harlequin® Special Edition novels and my 2 FREE gifts (gifts are worth about $10). After receiving them, if I don't wish to receive any more books, I can return the shipping statement marked "cancel." If I don't cancel, I will receive 6 brand-new novels every month and be billed just $4.49 per book in the U.S. or $5.24 per book in Canada. That's a saving of at least 14% off the cover price! It's quite a bargain! Shipping and handling is just 50¢ per book in the U.S. and 75¢ per book in Canada.* I understand that accepting the 2 free books and gifts places me under no obligation to buy anything. I can always return a shipment and cancel at any time. Even if I never buy another book, the two free books and gifts are mine to keep forever.

235/335 HDN FEGF

Name	(PLEASE PRINT)

Address	Apt. #

City	State/Prov.	Zip/Postal Code

Signature (if under 18, a parent or guardian must sign)

Mail to the **Reader Service:**
IN U.S.A.: P.O. Box 1867, Buffalo, NY 14240-1867
IN CANADA: P.O. Box 609, Fort Erie, Ontario L2A 5X3

Not valid for current subscribers to Harlequin Special Edition books.

Want to try two free books from another line?
Call 1-800-873-8635 or visit www.ReaderService.com.

* Terms and prices subject to change without notice. Prices do not include applicable taxes. Sales tax applicable in N.Y. Canadian residents will be charged applicable taxes. Offer not valid in Quebec. This offer is limited to one order per household. All orders subject to credit approval. Credit or debit balances in a customer's account(s) may be offset by any other outstanding balance owed by or to the customer. Please allow 4 to 6 weeks for delivery. Offer available while quantities last.

Your Privacy—The Reader Service is committed to protecting your privacy. Our Privacy Policy is available online at www.ReaderService.com or upon request from the Reader Service.

We make a portion of our mailing list available to reputable third parties that offer products we believe may interest you. If you prefer that we not exchange your name with third parties, or if you wish to clarify or modify your communication preferences, please visit us at www.ReaderService.com/consumerschoice or write to us at Reader Service Preference Service, P.O. Box 9062, Buffalo, NY 14269. Include your complete name and address.

HSE11B

*Harlequin Romantic Suspense presents the latest book
in the scorching new* KELLEY LEGACY *miniseries
from best-loved veteran series author Carla Cassidy*

*Scandal is the name of the game as the Kelley family fights
to preserve their legacy, their hearts...and their lives.*

Read on for an excerpt from the fourth title
RANCHER UNDER COVER

*Available October 2011
from Harlequin Romantic Suspense*

"**W**ould you like a drink?" Caitlin asked as she walked
to the minibar in the corner of the room. She felt as if she
needed to chug a beer or two for courage.

"No, thanks. I'm not much of a drinking man," he
replied.

She raised an eyebrow and looked at him curiously as she
poured herself a glass of wine. "A ranch hand who doesn't
enjoy a drink? I think maybe that's a first."

He smiled easily. "There was a six-month period in my
life when I drank too much. I pulled myself out of the bottom of a bottle a little over seven years ago and I've never
looked back."

"That's admirable, to know you have a problem and then
fix it."

Those broad shoulders of his moved up and down in
an easy shrug. "I don't know how admirable it was, all I
knew at the time was that I had a choice to make between
living and dying and I decided living was definitely more
appealing."

She wanted to ask him what had happened preceding
that six-month period that had plunged him into the bottom

of the bottle, but she didn't want to know too much about him. Personal information might produce a false sense of intimacy that she didn't need, didn't want in her life.

"Please, sit down," she said, and gestured him to the table. She had never felt so on edge, so awkward in her life.

"After you," he replied.

She was aware of his gaze intensely focused on her as she rounded the table and sat in the chair, and she wanted to tell him to stop looking at her as if she were a delectable dessert he intended to savor later.

Watch Caitlin and Rhett's sensual saga unfold amidst the shocking, ripped-from-the-headlines drama of the Kelley Legacy miniseries in

RANCHER UNDER COVER

Available October 2011 only from Harlequin Romantic Suspense, wherever books are sold.

Harlequin® SHOWCASE

2 GREAT NOVELS
1 GREAT PRICE

USA TODAY Bestselling Author

RaeAnne Thayne

**On the sun-swept sands of
Cannon Beach, Oregon, two couples
with guarded hearts search for
a second chance at love.**

Discover two classic stories of love and family
from the Women of Brambleberry House miniseries
in one incredible volume.

BRAMBLEBERRY SHORES

Available September 27, 2011.

www.Harlequin.com

HSC68836

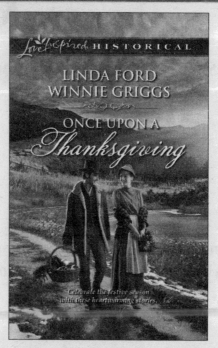